Tolstoy Bilingual

Edited by Tamara Eidelman and Lydia Razran Stone

Originally published as issue #20 of the journal *Chtenia*.

Special thanks to Susanna Nazarova for proofreading the Russian and its accenting.

Cover photo: Lev Tolstoy, 1908. Photo by Karl Bulla.

ISBN 978-1-880100-40-0

StoryWorkz, Inc.
73 Main Street, Suite 402
Montpelier, VT 05602
storyworkz.com

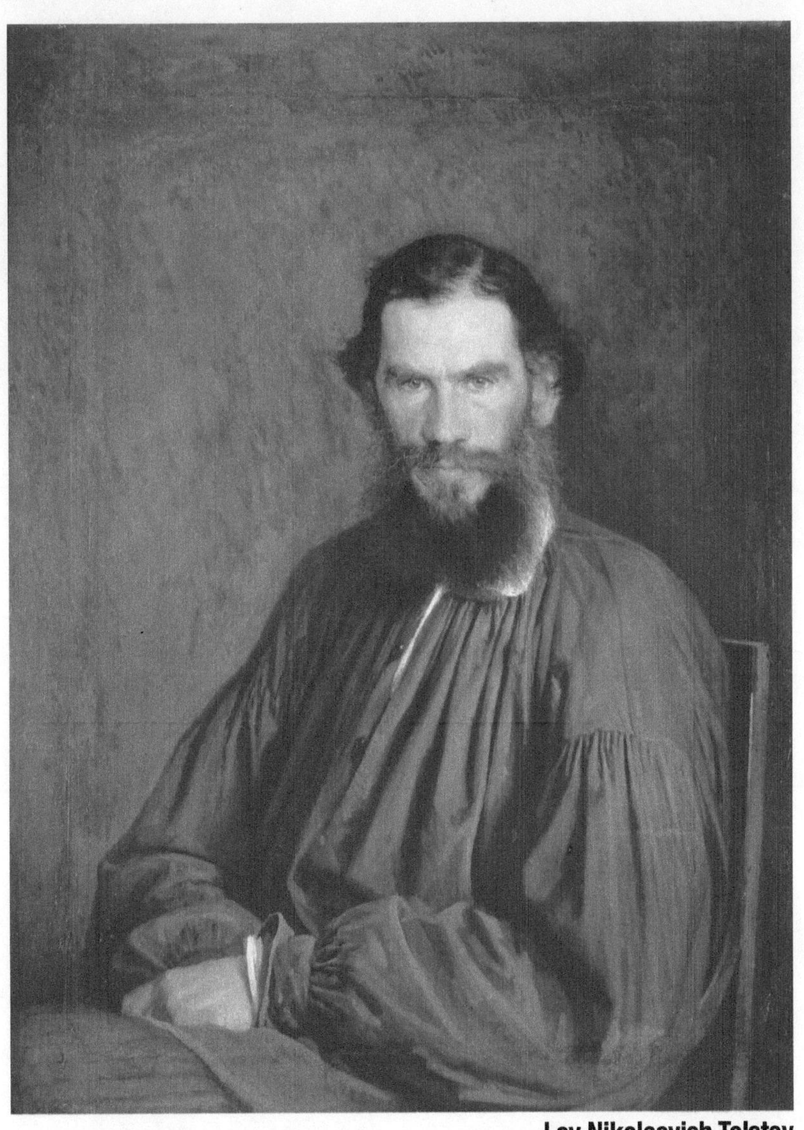

Lev Nikolaevich Tolstoy
Ivan Kramskoy (1873)

Contents

Leo and Lev
Lydia Razran Stone

If the term "literary genius" means anything at all, Lev (Leo) Nikolayevich Tolstoy was one; he was also unquestionably a Russian soul *par excellence*.

In the view of many, this combination would suggest that he was a man of many contradictions – and indeed he was. A consummate artist, toward the end of his life he rejected all art not immediately accessible to the most uneducated members of the population. Unequaled in his description of the joyful moments of life, he was obsessed with death and the meaninglessness of life for most of his own, and he suffered from depression. Although he produced some of the most striking battle scenes in world literature, he ultimately rejected war and violence of any kind. Tolstoy was famous for his celebrations of family happiness, yet his own relationship with his wife was contentious for decades and ultimately became unbearably so. A master of the use of well-structured logical argument to reject shibboleths, he pervasively espoused the idea that reason could not explain human experience or make sense of life. During the time he was (at the age of 60) writing a novella rejecting sexual

relations even within marriage, his wife was carrying his 13th child (her 16th pregnancy). A monumental egoist and autocrat to his family, he embraced living for the sake of others and humility as life principles. Years after devoting page after page to debunking the idea that a single "great" man could affect history, he founded a worldwide movement and was literally venerated by his followers.

Absolutely all of the above is profusely documented in print, if not in Tolstoy's literary works, then in his letters and diaries, not to mention those of the people surrounding him. Needless to say, it was quite a challenge to select material to even semi-adequately represent Tolstoy in a single bilingual issue. We did our best. The brief introduction to each excerpt, story or reading explains our choices.

About the translations. The final story, *Alyosha the Pot*, was translated by Michael Katz and *Bedbugs* was translated by Robert Blaisdell. The remaining stories were all translated by me. For a few of my translations I used only the Russian as a reference in translating. For the others I started with the Louise and Aylmer Maude translations of the early twentieth century. Yet I changed so much from their work that I feel justified in calling these original translations, while still acknowledging a debt to the very competent Maudes. However, as Joel Carmichael says in his afterword to the Bantam Classic Edition of his *Anna Karenina* translation (1960), "Tolstoy can pull his own weight: his translators merely need to clear the way."

In some cases I have added to the English a brief explanation when a literal translation of the Russian would not have the connotations for a general English reader that would have been automatic for Tolstoy's Russian audience. My translations were reviewed by my friend Diana Bailey Harris, who does not speak Russian, but is a wonderful writer and translates from Italian. She made suggestions for smoothing out my syntax when it got too Russian, and for substituting words – I accepted many of these and am very grateful for the improvements they made in my text. Readers should be aware that, although this is a bilingual issue,

it is not a line by line or word by word translation and thus, it may fail to tell you the exact meaning of some word encountered in the Russian text. We do hope and expect that it will tell you what Tolstoy was saying to his readers in any given sentence or paragraph.

About the image of Tolstoy in the United States. I own a fascinating book, *The Top Ten: Writers Pick Their Favorite Books*, edited by J. Peder Zane (W.W. Norton and Company; 2007). In it, 100 U.S. and British writers are asked to rank their all-time favorite reads. A compilation of all the responses shows *Anna Karenina* first and *War and Peace* third (*Madame Bovary* is second) out of all books ever written. When a list of top ten authors by rating points is computed, Tolstoy is first with 327 points and Shakespeare second with 293. Dostoyevsky is fourth with 177 and Chekhov eighth with 165. Quite a showing for the Russians among English speaking writers, and a clear demonstration that, among those who know (or at least the subset who write), the joy of reading Tolstoy is fully recognized.

For decades I have been collecting references to Tolstoy's masterpieces in U.S. media – mainly advertisements and comics – and know that, despite universal acknowledgement of Tolstoy's greatness, almost universally in this milieu his works are held up as the epitome of long, heavy, difficult and unreadable works, which a few snobs pretend to have actually read.[1] We hope that this volume will help to dispel the ridiculous myth that Tolstoy is unreadable, although most of our readers are undoubtedly too erudite ever to have believed that myth.

Finally, a personal note from the translator and curator of this issue. Almost exactly 50 years ago I was a teenager attending a small but ludicrously rigorous college. Two of us had convinced our marvelous old-world Russian teacher that, if we studied all summer, our Russian would

---

1. Perhaps the most amusing of all of these was an advertisement for medicine to treat "traveller's gastric distress." Under the general heading "Chance of reading on vacation" is a picture of a nineteenth century-looking volume of War and Peace in English, with a caption that reads "1 in 46." Below this is a picture of a package of diarrhea medicine, with the typical instructional verbiage on the carton; below this is written "1 in 3" and finally in somewhat larger letters "Pack Wisely."

be good enough for her to offer literature seminars in Russian. The first seminar that fall was on Tolstoy. After assigning us some short works, she gave us three weeks to read *War and Peace* (in the seminar system we had only one other class).

By the time I had finished, not only was I in love with Lev Nikolayevich, but I could read Russian without using a dictionary (except occasionally) and without translating in my head into English. I had gotten so carried away by the story that I simply inferred (a.k.a. guessed) the approximate meaning of words I did not know, the way a small child listening to a story containing unfamiliar language would.

I have therefore always been very grateful to Tolstoy for allowing me to develop this knack so early in my career as a Slavist and I am now grateful that this volume has given me the opportunity, at least in some small measure, to add to Tolstoy's reputation in return.

Contributors

LEV NIKOLAEVICH TOLSTOY (1828-1910) was born in Yasnaya Polyana as the fourth son of Maria Volkonsky and Count Nikolai Tolstoy. His mother died when he was just 18 months old and he and his brothers were mainly raised by aunts. Leaving Kazan University early, young Lev for a time led a rather dissolute and debauched life before following his brother Nicholas into the military, serving in the Caucasus before and during the Crimean War. Writing about these experiences launched his literary career.

Tolstoy primarily wrote novels and short stories. Later in life he focused more on didactic plays and essays. His two most famous works, the novels War and Peace and Anna Karenina, are widely acknowledged as two of the greatest novels of all time and pinnacles of realist fiction.

Tolstoy is equally known for his complicated personality and for his extreme moralism and asceticism, which he adopted after a moral crisis and spiritual awakening in the 1870s.

His literal interpretation of the ethical teachings of Jesus, centering on the Sermon on the Mount, caused him in later life to become a fervent Christian anarchist and anarcho-pacifist, and led to his excommunication from the Russian Orthodox Church. His ideas on nonviolent resistance, expressed in such works as The Kingdom of God Is Within You, were to have a profound impact on such pivotal twentieth-century figures as Mohandas Gandhi and

Martin Luther King, Jr.

Tolstoy's rejection of personal wealth and his long battle with his wife over the rights and royalties to his works eventually precipitated his sudden departure from Yasnaya Polyana in 1910, and his eventual death at the remote train station of Astapov (wonderfully dramatized in the novel The Last Station, by Jay Parini, and the film based on the book).

ROBERT BLAISDELL teaches writing and literature at the City University of New York's Kingsborough Community College in Brooklyn. He has edited more than thirty literary anthologies, including Tolstoy as Teacher: Leo Tolstoy's Writings on Education and The Wit and Wisdom of Abraham Lincoln. He occasionally reviews books for the San Francisco Chronicle and the Christian Science Monitor.

LYDIA RAZRAN STONE has translated and analyzed biomedical research for NASA, and edits SlavFile, the quarterly newsletter for Slavic translators. She has published three books of translated poetry, and has a forthcoming dictionary of English sports idioms. Her translation of Krylov's fairy tales, The Frogs Who Begged for a Tsar (and 61 other Russian fables by Ivan Krylov), was published by Russian Life Books in 2010. Her latest project involves English versions of the songs of Bulat Okudzhava.

This autobiographical description of what Tolstoy calls his oldest and dearest memory provides a preview of some of his deepest lifelong concerns. Here the five-year-old Tolstoy, orphaned too young to remember his mother, experiences a moment of transcendent and touching intimacy with his brothers as they play a game associated with discovering the magical key to making all men happy for eternity. As is characteristic of Tolstoy, the focus on emotions and philosophical aims merges with the description of charming if trivial details from everyday life – here his own.

Fanfaronov's Mountain (The Ant Brothers)
Leo Tolstoy

And then there was Fanfaronov's Mountain, one of my earliest, dearest and most significant memories. My oldest brother, Nikolenka, was 6 years older than I, so he must have been 10 or 11 when I was 4 or 5, and he introduced us to Fanfaronov's Mountain. I do not know exactly how this came about, but when we were very young we addressed him with the formal "you," as if he were an adult. He was a remarkable child and grew up to be a remarkable man. What an imagination he had! He would tell us fairy tales, ghost stories and comic yarns for hours on end, without faltering or pausing, and with such confidence in their reality that we simply forgot he had made them up.

When he wasn't telling stories or reading (he read a huge amount), he was drawing. Almost all his drawings were devils, with horns and fancy mustaches, linked together in the most fantastic poses and doing all kinds of remarkable things. Like his stories, his drawings were full of imagination and humor.

And it was he who – when my brothers and I were 5 (I), 6 (Mitenka) and 7 (Seryozha) – announced to us that he knew a secret that, when made

Фанфаро́нова гора́

Да, Фанфаро́нова гора́. Это одно́ из са́мых далёких и ми́лых и ва́жных воспомина́ний. Ста́рший брат Нико́ленька был на 6 лет ста́рше меня́. Ему́ бы́ло, ста́ло быть, 10-11, когда́ мне бы́ло 4 и́ли 5, и́менно когда́ он води́л нас на Фанфаро́нову го́ру. Мы в пе́рвой мо́лодости, не зна́ю, как э́то случи́лось, говори́ли ему́ "вы". Он был удиви́тельный ма́льчик и пото́м удиви́тельный челове́к. …Воображе́ние у него́ бы́ло тако́е, что он мог расска́зывать ска́зки и́ли исто́рии с привиде́ниями и́ли юмористи́ческие исто́рии … без остано́вки и запи́нки це́лыми часа́ми и с тако́й уве́ренностью в действи́тельность расска́зываемого, что забыва́лось, что э́то вы́думка.

Когда́ он не расска́зывал и не чита́л (он чита́л чрезвыча́йно мно́го), он рисова́л. Рисова́л он почти́ всегда́ черте́й с рога́ми, закру́ченными уса́ми, сцепля́ющихся в са́мых разнообра́зных по́зах ме́жду собо́ю и за́нятых са́мыми разнообра́зными дела́ми. Рису́нки э́ти то́же бы́ли полны́ воображе́ния и ю́мора.

Так во́т он-то, когда́ нам с бра́тьями бы́ло – мне 5, Ми́теньке 6, Серёже 7 лет, объяви́л нам, что у него́ есть та́йна, посре́дством кото́рой, когда́ она́ откро́ется, все лю́ди сде́лаются счастли́выми, не бу́дет ни боле́зней,

known to the world, would bring happiness to all people everywhere. No one would be sick or have any kind of trouble and no one would get angry at anyone else, because everyone would become "Ant Brothers." (Undoubtedly, he meant to refer to the Moravian Brothers, whom he had heard or read about, but to us they were the "Ant Brothers"[1]). And I remember that I was especially taken by the word "ant," since it made me think of ants all tumbled together in their cozy hill. We even made up an "Ant Brothers" game. We arranged crates all around some armchairs, which we had draped with scarves; then we all crawled in and huddled together in the dark. I remember feeling a unique surge of love and deep emotion when we did so. This was one of my favorite games.

Although the "Ant Brothers" secret had been revealed to us, we did not yet have the secret key to make it come to pass, such that people everywhere would no longer know the slightest unhappiness, would no longer fight with each other or even get angry, but instead be constantly and forever happy. We learned that the Brothers had written the secret words on a green stick and buried this stick at the edge of a ravine in the old forest preserve, at a spot where, since my body will have to be put somewhere, I have asked to be buried – in memory of Nikolenka.

However, there was more to the secret than even the green stick. There was also a place called Fanfaronov's[2] Mountain, where my brother promised to take us after we had performed a series of labors. The first was to sit in the corner and not think about a white bear. I remember sitting in the corner and trying, but I never could keep that white bear out of my head. I do not recall exactly what the second labor was, except that it was very difficult… something on the order of walking, without a false step, along the crack between two floorboards. The third task, on the other hand, seemed easy. For a whole year you had to keep from laying eyes on a rabbit, neither alive,

---

1. The Russian adjective for ant (muraveyny) sounds very much like the word for Moravian (Moravsky).

2. "Fanfaron" in Russian – based on the word for fanfare (fanfara) – is an exotic, French-sounding word that means something like swaggering or bragging.

никаки́х неприя́тностей, никто́ ни на кого́ не бу́дет серди́ться и все бу́дут люби́ть друг дру́га, все сде́лаются муравейными бра́тьями. (Вероя́тно, э́то бы́ли Мора́вские бра́тья, о кото́рых он слы́шал и́ли чита́л, но на на́шем языке́ э́то бы́ли муравейные бра́тья.) И я по́мню, что сло́во "муравейные" осо́бенно нра́вилось, напомина́я муравьёв в ко́чке. Мы да́же устро́или игру́ в муравейные бра́тья, кото́рая состоя́ла в том, что сади́лись под сту́лья, загора́живали их я́щиками, заве́шивали платка́ми и сиде́ли там в темноте́, прижима́ясь друг к дру́гу. Я, по́мню, испы́тывал осо́бенное чу́вство любви́ и умиле́ния и о́чень люби́л э́ту игру́.

Муравейное бра́тство бы́ло откры́то нам, но гла́вная та́йна о том, как сде́лать, что́бы все лю́ди не зна́ли никаки́х несча́стий, никогда́ не ссо́рились и не серди́лись, а бы́ли бы постоя́нно сча́стливы, э́та та́йна была́, как он нам говори́л, напи́сана им на зелёной па́лочке, и па́лочка э́та зары́та у доро́ги, на краю́ овра́га ста́рого Зака́за, в том ме́сте, в кото́ром я, та́к как на́до же где́-нибудь зары́ть мой труп, проси́л в па́мять Нико́леньки закопа́ть меня́.

Кро́ме э́той па́лочки, была́ ещё кака́я-то Фанфаро́нова гора́, на кото́рую, он говори́л, что мо́жет ввести́ нас, е́сли то́лько мы испо́лним все поло́женные для того́ усло́вия. Усло́вия бы́ли, во-пе́рвых, стать в у́гол и не ду́мать о бе́лом медве́де. По́мню, как я станови́лся в у́гол и стара́лся, но ника́к не мог не ду́мать о бе́лом медве́де. Второ́е усло́вие я не по́мню, како́е-то о́чень тру́дное... пройти́, не оступи́вшись, по щёлке ме́жду полови́цами, и тре́тье лёгкое: в продолже́ние го́да не вида́ть за́йца, всё равно, живо́го, и́ли мёртвого, и́ли жа́реного. Пото́м на́до покля́сться никому́ не открыва́ть э́тих тайн.

nor dead, nor even roasted. After that, you had to swear not to reveal these secrets to anyone.

Any boy who performed these labors, and others even more difficult, which Nikolenka was going to tell us about later, would be granted one wish, no matter what it was. We were required to reveal our wishes. Seryosha wanted to be able to sculpt horses and chickens out of wax. Mitenka wanted to be able to draw everything as big as life, like a real artist. I myself couldn't think of anything to wish for other than to be able to draw things too, but on a smaller scale. As almost always happens with children, we very soon forgot all this, and no one ever climbed Fanfaronov's Mountain, but I can still remember the grave and mysterious air with which Nikolenka shared these secrets with us, and our respect and awe for the remarkable things that had been revealed to us.

But what made the strongest impression on me was the "Ant Brotherhood" and the green stick mysteriously linked to it that was destined to create happiness for all people everywhere. I now assume that Nikolenka had read or heard of the Masons, whose goal was happiness for all humanity, and about the mysterious rites of initiation into their order, as well as about the Moravian Brotherhood, and had undoubtedly combined all this in his own vivid imagination with his love of humanity and inate kindness, and had made up these stories, which delighted him and beguiled us.

The ideal of the "Ant Brothers," lovingly clinging to each other, although not under two arm chairs draped with scarves, but under the vast sky sheltering everyone in the world, has remained with me unaltered. I still believe today, just as I believed then, in the green stick bearing an inscription destined to annihilate all that is evil in humanity and deliver blissful happiness. That is, I believe such wisdom exists and, when it is revealed to humanity, its promise will be fulfilled.

First published in Russian: 1847
Translation by Lydia Razran Stone

Тот, кто испо́лнит э́ти усло́вия, и ещё други́е, бо́лее тру́дные, кото́рые он откро́ет по́сле, того́ одно́ жела́ние, како́е бы оно́ ни́ было, бу́дет испо́лнено. Мы должны́ бы́ли сказа́ть на́ши жела́ния. Серёжа пожела́л уме́ть лепи́ть лошаде́й и кур из во́ска, Ми́тенька пожела́л уме́ть рисова́ть вся́кие ве́щи, как живопи́сец, в большо́м ви́де. Я же ничего́ не мог приду́мать, кро́ме того́, что́бы уме́ть рисова́ть в ма́лом ви́де. Всё э́то, как э́то быва́ет у дете́й, о́чень ско́ро забы́лось, и никто́ не вошёл на Фанфаро́нову го́ру, но по́мню ту тайнственную ва́жность, с кото́рой Нико́ленька посвяща́л нас в э́ти та́йны, и на́ше уваже́ние и тре́пет пе́ред те́ми удиви́тельными веща́ми, кото́рые нам открыва́лись.

В осо́бенности же оста́вило во мне си́льное впечатле́ние муравѐйное бра́тство и тайнственная зелёная па́лочка, свя́зывавшаяся с ним и долженству́ющая осчастли́вить всех люде́й. Как тепе́рь я ду́маю, Нико́ленька, вероя́тно, прочёл и́ли наслу́шался о масо́нах, об их стремле́нии к осчастли́влению челове́чества, о тайнственных обря́дах приёма в их о́рден, вероя́тно, слы́шал о Мора́вских бра́тьях и соедини́л всё э́то в одно́ в своём живо́м воображе́нии и любви́ к лю́дям, к доброте́, приду́мал все э́ти исто́рии и сам ра́довался им и моро́чил и́ми нас.

Идеа́л муравѐйных бра́тьев, льну́щих любо́вно друг к дру́гу, то́лько не под двумя́ кре́слами, заве́шанными платка́ми, а под всем небе́сным сво́дом всех люде́й ми́ра, оста́лся для меня́ тот же. И как я тогда́ ве́рил, что есть та зелёная па́лочка, на кото́рой напи́сано то, что должно́ уничто́жить всё зло в лю́дях и дать им вели́кое бла́го, так я ве́рю и тепе́рь, что есть э́та и́стина и что бу́дет она́ откры́та лю́дям и даст им то, что она́ обеща́ет.

This story, published in 1863, is one of several that Tolstoy set in the Caucasus – the "wild west" of nineteenth century Russia. Tolstoy served in the Caucasus in the 1850's and had the kind of army adventures young men dream of – as does his hero Olenin. This excerpt is notable for two reasons. First it provides a first glimpse of the kind of emotional stream of consciousness that is such a brilliant feature of Tolstoy's style. Second, it is one of the many passages in his work devoted to the emotional effects of natural beauty. Tolstoy breaks with romantic tradition by describing such phenomena not in flowery and detailed phrases, but in terms of the overwhelming effects they have on his characters – here described in a particularly effective yet linguistically simple and un-flowery manner.

The Cossacks

Chapter 3

The further Olenin got from central Russia, the more remote his memories seemed; the closer he got to the Caucasus the more light-hearted he felt. The thought that he might just stay away for good and never again show his face in Moscow society kept popping into his mind. "The people I see here do not matter; none of them know me, none would ever come to Moscow and move in my circle or learn about my past, and certainly no one from my circle will ever know anything about what I do here, living among these people." A completely unaccustomed feeling of freedom, of having shed his past, washed over him at finding himself among the uncouth types he saw on the road, whom he did not consider to matter the way his Moscow acquaintances did. The more uncouth the people appeared and the fewer the signs of civilization, the more liberated he felt. Yet his gloom returned when he had to pass through Stavropol. The sight of the signboards, some even in French, the ladies in fancy carriages, the coaches in the square, and an elegantly-dressed gentleman strolling along the boulevard, who looked him up and down as he rode by, caused him real pain. "What if these people and I have acquaintances in common?" he thought. And his mind returned again to his club, his unpaid tailor, his gambling debts, and the opinion of

Казаки

III

Чем да́льше уезжа́л Оле́нин от це́нтра Росси́и, тем да́льше каза́лись от него́ все его́ воспомина́ния, и чем бли́же подъезжа́л к Кавка́зу, тем отра́днее станови́лось ему́ на душе́. «Уе́хать совсе́м и никогда́ не приезжа́ть наза́д, не пока́зываться в о́бщество,– приходи́ло ему́ иногда́ в го́лову, – А э́ти лю́ди, кото́рых я здесь ви́жу, не лю́ди, никто́ из них меня́ не зна́ет и никто́ никогда́ не мо́жет быть в Москве́ в том о́бществе, где я был, и узна́ть о моём проше́дшем. И никто́ из того́ о́бщества не узна́ет, что я де́лал, живя́ ме́жду э́тими людьми́». И соверше́нно но́вое для него́ чу́вство свобо́ды от всего́ проше́дшего охва́тывало его́ ме́жду э́тими гру́быми существа́ми, кото́рых он встреча́л по доро́ге и кото́рых не признава́л людьми́ наравне́ с свои́ми моско́вскими знако́мыми. Чем грубе́е был наро́д, чем ме́ньше бы́ло при́знаков цивилиза́ции, тем свобо́днее он чу́вствовал себя́. Ста́врополь, чрез кото́рый он до́лжен был проезжа́ть, огорчи́л его́. Вы́вески, да́же францу́зские вы́вески, да́мы в коля́ске, изво́зчики, стоя́вшие на пло́щади, бульва́р и господи́н в шине́ли и шля́пе, проходи́вший по бульва́ру и огляде́вший прое́зжего,– бо́льно поде́йствовали на него́. «Мо́жет быть, э́ти лю́ди зна́ют кого́-нибудь из мои́х знако́мых»,– и ему́ опя́ть вспо́мнились клуб, портно́й, ка́рты, свет...

Moscow society. But once Stavropol was behind him, there were no more painful reminders and everything pleased him. His surroundings seemed not merely wild, but beautiful, and somehow warlike; his mood grew more and more cheerful. The Cossacks, stage drivers, and stationmasters seemed to him simple souls with whom he could joke and say whatever he liked, without needing to adjust his words to the social class they belonged to. After all, all these people belonged to the human race, all of whose members Olenin, without consciously thinking about it, felt kindly toward; and all of them responded to him in a friendly manner.

Earlier, while they were still in Don Cossack territory, the sleigh they were traveling in had had to be replaced with a stagecoach and, after they passed Stavropol, it was so warm that Olenin shed his fur coat. It was already spring here – an unanticipated, light-hearted spring for Olenin. Travelers were not permitted to venture out of stagecoach stations at night; even in the evening travel was said to be dangerous. Vanyusha[1] became nervous and a loaded rifle was kept close at hand in the coach. Olenin's high spirits increased even further. At one of the stops, the station master told him of a terrible murder recently committed on the high road. They began to encounter armed men. "Ah, so this is where it all starts!" Olenin thought. At any moment he expected to see the snow-covered mountains that everyone had so much to say about. Once, towards evening, the Nogay driver pointed his whip at something barely visible behind clouds. Olenin avidly strained his eyes, but the day was overcast and the mountain was half obscured by clouds. Olenin saw only something grey and white and fleecy, but, in spite of his best efforts, he was unable to find anything wonderful in the sight of these mountains, about which he had heard and read so much. He decided the mountains looked like just another cloud formation and that the oft-praised special beauty of snow-covered mountains was the same kind of fabrication as the magnificence of Bach's music or a woman's love, neither of which he believed in. Thus, he no longer eagerly anticipated seeing the

---

1. Olenin's servant.

От Ста́врополя зато́ всё уже́ пошло́ удовлетвори́тельно: ди́ко и сверх того́ краси́во и войнственно. И Оле́нину всё станови́лось веселе́е и веселе́е. Все каза́ки,[1] ямщики́, смотри́теля каза́лись ему́ просты́ми существа́ми, с кото́рыми ему́ мо́жно бы́ло про́сто шути́ть, бесе́довать, не сообража́я, кто к како́му разря́ду принадлежи́т. Все принадлежа́ли к ро́ду челове́ческому, кото́рый был весь бессозна́тельно мил Оле́нину, и все дружелю́бно относи́лись к нему́.

Ещё в Земле́ Во́йска Донско́го перемени́ли са́ни на теле́гу; а за Ста́врополем уже́ ста́ло так тепло́, что Оле́нин е́хал без шу́бы. Была́ уже́ весна́ – неожи́данная, весёлая весна́ для Оле́нина. Но́чью уже́ не пуска́ли из стани́ц и ве́чером говори́ли, что опа́сно. Ваню́ша стал потру́шивать, и ружьё заря́женное лежа́ло на перекладно́й. Оле́нин стал ещё веселе́е. На одно́й ста́нции смотри́тель рассказа́л неда́вно случи́вшееся стра́шное убийство на доро́ге. Ста́ли встреча́ться вооружённые лю́ди. «Вот оно́ где начина́ется!» – говори́л себе́ Оле́нин и всё ждал ви́да снеговы́х гор, про кото́рые мно́го говори́ли ему́. Оди́н ра́з, пе́ред ве́чером, нога́ец-ямщи́к пле́тью указа́л из-за туч на го́ры. Оле́нин с жа́дностью стал вгля́дываться, но бы́ло па́смурно и облака́ до полови́ны застила́ли го́ры. Оле́нину видне́лось что́-то се́рое, бе́лое, курча́вое, и, как он ни стара́лся, он не мог найти́ ничего́ хоро́шего в ви́де гор, про кото́рые он сто́лько чита́л и слы́шал. Он поду́мал, что го́ры и облака́ име́ют соверше́нно одина́ковый вид и что осо́бенная красота́ снеговы́х гор, о кото́рых ему́ толкова́ли, есть така́я же вы́думка, как му́зыка Ба́ха и любо́вь к же́нщине, в кото́рые он не ве́рил, – и он переста́л дожида́ться гор. Но на друго́й день, ра́но у́тром, он проснулся от свѣ́жести в

1. Tolstoy used a specific accenting on the second syllable of каза́ки, which students of Russian will know is contra to the current standard: казаки́.

mountains. But early the next morning a chill in the air woke him in the stage and he glanced casually to his right. The morning was absolutely clear. Suddenly, he saw gigantic, pure white masses marked with delicate relief and the fantastic, clearly defined, airy outlines of the peaks against the sky, which at first glance looked to be a mere twenty paces away. When he realized how far away the mountains and the sky actually were, and how immense the mountains were and had assimilated their inexhaustible beauty, he was actually frightened, afraid that this was a vision or a dream. However, though he tried to shake himself awake, the mountains remained exactly as they had been.

"What's that? What's that over there?" he asked the driver.

"Why, the mountains," answered the Nogay driver in an offhand way.

"I've been looking at them myself for quite a while," said Vanyusha. "They're fantastic! No one at home would believe me if I told them."

The rapid pace of the troika along the smooth road made the mountains look as if they were sliding along the horizon, their pinkish peaks gleaming in the rising sun. At first, the mountains merely astonished Olenin; then they delighted him. He continued to gaze at the chain of snow-covered peaks, which seemed to rise up – not from among the black mountains, but directly out of the steppe – and to glide away into the distance. Little by little, he began to assimilate their beauty and finally to experience the mountains fully. From that moment on, everything he saw, everything he thought and felt, seemed to partake of the stern majesty of the mountains. His Moscow memories, his shame and remorse, his petty vulgar dreams about the Caucasus, all vanished, never to return. "Now it has begun," he imagined he heard a solemn voice say. The road and the line of the Terek River, visible in the distance, the Cossack villages and people, no longer seemed of little significance to real life. He looked at the sky – and remembered the mountains. He looked down at himself or across at Vanyusha... again, there were the mountains. Two Cossacks rode by, the rifles on their backs rhythmically posting up and down, the white and bay legs of their horses appearing to belong to a single animal... and there were

свое́й перекладно́й и равноду́шно взгляну́л напра́во. У́тро было совершенно я́сное. Вдруг он увида́л, шага́х в двадцати́ от себя́, как ему́ показа́лось в пе́рвую мину́ту, чи́сто-бе́лые грома́ды с их не́жными очерта́ниями и причу́дливую, отчётливую возду́шную ли́нию их верши́н и далёкого не́ба. И когда́ он по́нял всю даль ме́жду им и гора́ми и не́бом, всю грома́дность гор, и когда́ почу́вствовалась ему́ вся бесконе́чность э́той красоты́, он испуга́лся, что э́то при́зрак, сон. Он встряхну́лся, что́бы просну́ться. Го́ры бы́ли всё те же.

–Что э́то? Что э́то тако́е? – спроси́л он у ямщика́.

–А го́ры,– отвеча́л равноду́шно нога́ец.

–И я то́же давно́ на них смотрю́,– сказа́л Ваню́ша,– вот хорошо́-то! До́ма не пове́рят.

На бы́стром движе́нии тро́йки по ро́вной доро́ге го́ры, каза́лось, бежа́ли по горизо́нту, блестя́ на восходя́щем со́лнце свои́ми розова́тыми верши́нами. Снача́ла го́ры то́лько удиви́ли Оле́нина, пото́м обра́довали; но пото́м, бо́льше и бо́льше вгля́дываясь в э́ту, не из други́х чёрных гор, но пря́мо из сте́пи выраста́ющую и убега́ющую цепь снегов́ых гор, он ма́ло-пома́лу на́чал вника́ть в э́ту красоту́ и почу́вствовал го́ры. С э́той мину́ты всё, что то́лько он ви́дел, всё, что он ду́мал, всё, что он чу́вствовал, получа́ло для него́ но́вый, стро́го велича́вый хара́ктер гор. Все моско́вские воспомина́ния, стыд и раска́яние, все по́шлые мечты́ о Кавка́зе, все исче́зли и не возвраща́лись бо́лее. «Тепе́рь начало́сь»,– как бу́дто сказа́л ему́ како́й-то торже́ственный го́лос. И доро́га, и вдали́ видне́вшаяся черта́ Те́река, и стани́цы, и наро́д – всё э́то ему́ каза́лось тепе́рь уже́ не шу́ткой. Взгля́нет на не́бо – и вспо́мнит го́ры. Взгля́нет на себя́, на Ваню́шу – и опя́ть го́ры. Вот е́дут два каза́ка ве́рхом, и ру́жья в чехла́х равноме́рно пома́тываются у них за спи́нами, и ло́шади их переме́шиваются гнед́ыми и се́рыми нога́ми; а

the mountains! Beyond the Terek, smoke drifted up from a Tatar village... and there were the mountains! The sun rose, glistening on the river, visible through the reeds... and there were the mountains! A Tatar wagon emerged from the village, and women were walking by, young, beautiful women... and there were the mountains.

"Abreks prowl the steppe, but I ride along and do not fear them! I have my gun, and my strength, and my youth... and there are the mountains..."

First published in Russian: 1863
Translation by Lydia Razran Stone

горы... За Тереком виден дым в ауле; а горы... Солнце всходит и блещет на виднеющемся из-за камыша Тереке; а горы... Из станицы едет арба, женщины ходят красивые, женщины молодые; а горы... Абреки рыскают в степи, и я еду, их не боюсь, у меня ружьё, и сила, и молодость; а горы...

Here we meet Tolstoy's darling, Natasha Rostova, who throughout *War and Peace* serves as the embodiment of the joy and beauty of the Life Force. Unfortunately, in this chapter we observe her falling prey to a (thankfully transitory) period of corruption. This extract clearly and comically shows Tolstoy's contempt for the conventions and pretensions of high society and his trademark technique of остранение – *ostraneniye*, roughly translatable as "making strange" – describing a complex social or other phenomena as if through the eyes of a complete innocent, a person from a primitive culture, perhaps, or a child.

Natasha at the Opera

War and Peace
Volume II, Part V

8

Painted cardboard meant to represent trees stood around the sides of the stage; the floor was laid with wood boards of equal width and someone had stretched canvas over a frame in the back. A number of girls in red bodices and white skirts sat around the space at the center. Another, very fat, girl in a white silk dress sat apart on a low bench with green cardboard glued to its back. They were all singing something. When they finished, the girl in white walked toward the prompter's box and a man – in tight silk pants that hugged his fat legs and a costume that featured a feather and a dagger – approached her and began to sing and wave his arms.

The man in tight pants sang by himself at first; then the girl in white began. Then both were silent, while the orchestra continued to play and the man tapped his fingers on the girl's hand, evidently marking time until they were to begin singing again. Then they sang together and everyone in the theater began to clap and shout, and the man and

Ната́ша в о́пере

Война́ и мир
Том II, Часть V

8

На сце́не бы́ли ро́вные до́ски по среди́не, с боко́в стоя́ли кра́шеные карти́ны, изобража́вшие дере́вья, позади́ бы́ло протя́нуто полотно́ на до́сках. В середи́не сце́ны сиде́ли деви́цы в кра́сных корса́жах и бе́лых ю́бках. Одна́, о́чень то́лстая, в шёлковом бе́лом пла́тье, сиде́ла особо на ни́зкой скаме́ечке, к кото́рой был прикле́ен сза́ди зелёный карто́н. Все они́ пе́ли что-то. Когда́ они́ ко́нчили свою́ пе́сню, деви́ца в бе́лом подошла́ к бу́дочке суфлёра, и к ней подошёл мужчи́на в шёлковых, в обтя́жку, панталóнах на то́лстых нога́х, с перо́м и кинжа́лом и стал петь и разводи́ть рука́ми.

Мужчи́на в обтя́нутых панталóнах пропе́л оди́н, пото́м пропе́ла она́. Пото́м о́ба замо́лкли, заигра́ла му́зыка, и мужчи́на стал перебира́ть па́льцами ру́ку деви́цы в бе́лом пла́тье, очеви́дно выжида́я опя́ть та́кта, чтобы нача́ть свою́ па́ртию вме́сте с не́ю. Они́ пропе́ли вдвоём, и все в теа́тре ста́ли хло́пать и крича́ть, а мужчи́на и

woman on stage, who were meant to represent lovers, stood smiling and taking bows, arms outspread.

Natasha had returned from the country in such a serious mood that she found all this bewildering and grotesque. She was unable to follow the plot of the opera or even to listen to the music. All she perceived was painted cardboard and strangely dressed men and women, who moved, spoke and sang in an affected manner under bright lights. She knew what this was supposed to represent, but it was all so pretentiously false and artificial that she alternated between wanting to laugh at the performers and feeling embarrassed for them. She looked around at faces in the audience, searching for signs that they felt the same derision and confusion as she. However, the faces showed only attention to the action on stage, and delight, which she assumed was feigned. *No doubt this is the way it is supposed to be!* she thought. She kept looking around at the rows of pomaded men's heads in the orchestra seats and then at the half-naked women in the boxes. Her gaze was drawn back, again and again, to Hélène in the next box, who, with upper body quite exposed and a serene and gentle smile on her face, never took her eyes off the stage. And Natasha, responding to the bright light flooding the hall and the air made warm by the presence of the crowd, gradually began to pass into a dream-state such as she had not experienced for a long time. She was quite unaware of who she was, where she was, and what was going on in front of her. Her gaze fixed, she let her mind run free, and the strangest ideas – unexpected and disjointed – passed through her head. First she contemplated jumping onto the apron of the stage to sing the aria along with the fat girl in the white dress. Then she had the urge to poke an old man sitting nearby with her fan, and then she thought of leaning over toward Hélène and tickling her.[1]

Just when everything on stage was silent, anticipating the start of an aria, she heard the door of the box next to theirs creak, and then a man's footsteps. "Here's Kuragin!" whispered Shinshin. Smiling, Countess

1. Hélène's more formal name is Countess Bezhukhov. She is married to Pierre (who at this point in the story disdains her). She is also Anatole Kuragin's sister.

же́нщина на сце́не, кото́рые изобража́ли влюблённых, ста́ли, улыба́ясь и разводя́ рука́ми, кла́няться.

По́сле дере́вни и в том серьёзном настрое́нии, в кото́ром находи́лась Ната́ша, всё э́то бы́ло ди́ко и удиви́тельно ей. Она́ не могла́ следи́ть за хо́дом о́перы, не могла́ да́же слы́шать му́зыку: она́ ви́дела то́лько кра́шеные карто́ны и стра́нно-наря́женных мужчи́н и же́нщин, при я́рком све́те стра́нно дви́гавшихся, говори́вших и пе́вших; она́ зна́ла, что всё э́то должно́ бы́ло представля́ть, но всё э́то бы́ло так вы́чурно-фальши́во и ненатура́льно, что ей станови́лось то со́вестно за актёров, то смешно́ на них. Она́ огля́дывалась вокру́г себя́, на ли́ца зри́телей, оты́скивая в них то же чу́вство насме́шки и недоуме́ния, кото́рое бы́ло в ней; но все ли́ца бы́ли внима́тельны к тому́, что происходи́ло на сце́не и выража́ли притво́рное, как каза́лось Ната́ше, восхище́ние. «Должно́ быть э́то так на́добно!» ду́мала Ната́ша. Она́ попереме́нно огля́дывалась то на э́ти ряды́ припома́женных голо́в в парте́ре, то на оголённых же́нщин в ло́жах, в осо́бенности на свою́ сосе́дку Эле́н, кото́рая, соверше́нно разде́тая, с ти́хой и споко́йной улы́бкой, не спуска́я глаз, смотре́ла на сце́ну, ощуща́я я́ркий свет, разли́тый по всей за́ле и тёплый, толпо́ю согре́тый во́здух. Ната́ша ма́ло-по-ма́лу начина́ла приходи́ть в давно́ не испы́танное е́ю состоя́ние опьяне́ния. Она́ не по́мнила, что она́ и где она́ и что пе́ред ней де́лается. Она́ смотре́ла и ду́мала, и са́мые стра́нные мы́сли неожи́данно, без свя́зи, мелька́ли в её голове́. То ей приходи́ла мысль вскочи́ть на ра́мпу и пропе́ть ту а́рию, кото́рую пе́ла актри́са, то ей хоте́лось зацепи́ть ве́ером недалеко́ от неё сиде́вшего старичка́, то перегну́ться к Эле́н и защекота́ть её.

В одну́ из мину́т, когда́ на сце́не всё зати́хло, ожида́я нача́ла а́рии, скри́пнула входна́я дверь парте́ра, на той стороне́ где была́ ло́жа Росто́вых, и зазвуча́ли шаги́ запозда́вшего мужчи́ны. «Вот он Кура́гин!» прошепта́л Ши́ншин. Графи́ня Безу́хова улыба́ясь

Bezukhov turned to the latecomer. Natasha followed the Countess's eyes with her own, and saw an exceptionally handsome adjutant approaching the box with a self-confident, but, at the same time, courteous air. It was Anatole Kuragin, who had attracted her attention at a ball in St. Petersburg long ago. He now wore an adjutant's uniform with a single epaulette and a shoulder knot. He moved with a restrained swagger that would have been ridiculous had he not been so good-looking and had his handsome face not worn an expression of such good-humored self-assurance and high spirits. Although the performance was already in progress, he made no attempt to hurry, but walked nonchalantly down the carpeted hallway, his handsome, perfumed head held high and his spurs and saber rattling a bit. Glancing at Natasha, he went over to his sister, put his tightly gloved hand on the edge of her box, nodded, and, leaning closer, asked her something, indicating Natasha with a motion of his head.

"*Mais charmante!*"[2] he said, evidently referring to Natasha, who did not actually hear the words but read them as they formed on his lips. He then strolled to his place in the first row of the orchestra and sat down beside Dolokhov, nudging him with his elbow in a friendly and causal way. This was the same Dolokhov others treated with such sycophantic deference. Winking merrily, he smiled at him, then put his foot up on the apron of the stage.

"Doesn't he look just like his sister?" remarked Count Rostov. "And how good-looking they both are!"

Shinshin, lowering his voice, began to tell the count about one of Kuragin's intrigues in Moscow. Natasha tried to hear what he was saying, which she would never have done had he not just declared her "*charmante.*"

The first act came to an end. Everyone in the orchestra rose and began leaving and entering and generally milling about.

---

2. "But she is charming!"

обернулась к входящему. Наташа посмотрела по направлению глаз графини Безуховой и увидала необыкновенно красивого адъютанта, с самоуверенным и вместе учтивым видом подходящего к их ложе. Это был Анатоль Курагин, которого она давно видела и заметила на петербургском бале. Он был теперь в адъютантском мундире с одной эполетой и эксельбантом. Он шёл сдержанной, молодецкой походкой, которая была бы смешна, ежели бы он не был так хорош собой и ежели бы на прекрасном лице не было бы такого выражения добродушного довольства и веселия. Несмотря на то, что действие шло, он, не торопясь, слегка побрякивая шпорами и саблей, плавно и высоко неся свою надушенную красивую голову, шёл по ковру коридора. Взглянув на Наташу, он подошёл к сестре, положил руку в облитой перчатке на край её ложи, тряхнул ей головой и наклонясь спросил что-то, указывая на Наташу.

– *Mais charmante!* – сказал он, очевидно про Наташу, как не столько слышала она, сколько поняла по движению его губ. Потом он прошёл в первый ряд и сел подле Долохова, дружески и небрежно толкнув локтем того Долохова, с которым так заискивающе обращались другие. Он, весело подмигнув, улыбнулся ему и упёрся ногой в рампу.

– Как похожи брат с сестрой! – сказал граф. – И как хороши оба!

Шиншин вполголоса начал рассказывать графу какую-то историю интриги Курагина в Москве, к которой Наташа прислушалась именно потому, что он сказал про неё *charmante*.

Первый акт кончился, в партере все встали, перепутались и стали ходить и выходить.

Boris[3] came to the Rostovs' box and very gracefully accepted their congratulations on his engagement. He raised his eyebrows and smiled vaguely as he conveyed to Natasha and Sonya his fiancée's invitation to their wedding and then he left. This was the man with whom Natasha had so recently felt herself in love; yet she smiled gaily and flirtatiously while chatting with him and congratulating him on his engagement. Everything seemed simple and natural in her current state of dreamy intoxication. Hélène favored everyone without exception with her own particular smile; the smile Natasha now gave Boris looked exactly like Hélène's.

Men, the most well-known and witty in Moscow society, thronged to Hélène's box. The overflow crowded around the doorway, as if competing to announce to the world that they, too, were well acquainted with her.

Throughout the intermission, Kuragin stood with Dolokhov in front of the stage, gazing up at the Rostovs' box. Natasha knew he was talking about her and this gave her some satisfaction. She even turned her head in order to display her profile to him at what she believed was its best angle. She caught sight of Pierre[4] in the orchestra before the second act began. The Rostovs had not seen him since they arrived in Moscow. His face looked sad and he was even fatter than the last time Natasha had seen him. He walked toward the front of the theater without acknowledging anyone. Anatole came up and began talking to him, while continuing to gaze up at the Rostov's box. Pierre perked up when he saw Natasha, and hurried along the rows of seats to their box. Then he spent a long time chatting with Natasha, leaning on his elbows. As she talked to Pierre, Natasha heard a man's voice in Hélène's box and sensed that it was Kuragin's. She looked around and their eyes met. He gave a half-smile and looked directly into her eyes with such an enamored and tender look that she did not comprehend how she could be looking at him at such a close distance and be so absolutely certain that he was taken with her, when she had never even been introduced to him.

....

3. The son of a poor relation of the Rostov's, with whom Natasha had once thought herself in love.

4. Pierre Bezukhov, one of the two major heroes of the novel. At his point he is in love with Natasha, while she considers him a kindly uncle figure.

Борис пришёл в ложу Ростовых, очень просто принял поздравления и, приподняв брови, с рассеянной улыбкой, передал Наташе и Соне просьбу его невесты, чтобы они были на её свадьбе, и вышел. Наташа с весёлой и кокетливой улыбкой разговаривала с ним и поздравляла с женитьбой того самого Бориса, в которого она была влюблена прежде. В том состоянии опьянения, в котором она находилась, всё казалось просто и естественно.

Голая Элен сидела подле неё и одинаково всем улыбалась; и точно так же улыбнулась Наташа Борису.

Ложа Элен наполнилась и окружилась со стороны партера самыми знатными и умными мужчинами, которые, казалось, наперерыв желали показать всем, что они знакомы с ней.

Курагин весь этот антракт стоял с Долоховым впереди у рампы, глядя на ложу Ростовых. Наташа знала, что он говорил про неё, и это доставляло ей удовольствие. Она даже повернулась так, чтобы ему виден был её профиль, по её понятиям, в самом выгодном положении. Перед началом второго акта в партере показалась фигура Пьера, которого ещё с приезда не видали Ростовы. Лицо его было грустно, и он ещё потолстел, с тех пор как его последний раз видела Наташа. Он, никого не замечая, прошёл в первые ряды. Анатоль подошёл к нему и стал что-то говорить ему, глядя и указывая на ложу Ростовых. Пьер, увидав Наташу, оживился и поспешно, по рядам, пошёл к их ложе. Подойдя к ним, он облокотился и улыбаясь долго говорил с Наташей. Во время своего разговора с Пьером, Наташа услыхала в ложе графини Безуховой мужской голос и почему-то узнала, что это был Курагин. Она оглянулась и встретилась с ним глазами. Он почти улыбаясь смотрел ей прямо в глаза таким восхищённым, ласковым взглядом, что казалось странно быть от него так близко, так смотреть на него, быть так уверенной, что нравишься ему, и не быть с ним знакомой.

In the second act there were some pieces of cardboard on the stage meant to represent tombstones; a round hole in the canvas at the back was meant to be the moon; and the footlights were shaded. Trumpets and double basses began to play in the bass range as a number of people wearing black cloaks came in from left and right. With what looked like daggers in their hands, they began to wave their arms; then some different people ran in and began to drag away the girl who had worn the white dress before, but now had on a blue one. They did not accomplish this immediately, but spent quite some time singing with her and then finally dragged her off, while someone offstage beat on something metallic. Then all the people remaining on stage fell to their knees and began to sing something meant to be a prayer. All these actions were interrupted several times by ecstatic cheering from the audience.

Throughout this act, Natasha saw Anatole Kuragin each time she glanced down at the orchestra. He was gazing at her, with one arm draped over the back of his seat. She felt pleased that he was so captivated by her; it never entered her head that there was anything wrong about all of this.

Countess Bezukhova rose when the second act was over and turned to the Rostovs' box, with her entire bosom exposed; she beckoned to the old count with a gloved finger. Paying no attention to anyone else who came to her box, she began talking with him, smiling graciously.

"Please introduce me to your charming daughters," she said. "The whole town is singing their praises and I alone have not yet met them."

Natasha rose and curtsied to the magnificent countess. Such praise from this stunning beauty so delighted her that she blushed with pleasure.

"They make me wish that I, too, lived in Moscow," said Hélène. "You should be ashamed to bury such pearls in the country!"

Countess Bezukhova truly deserved her reputation as a fascinating woman. She could say things she did not mean – especially things that were flattering – quite simply and naturally.

"Do not argue, my dear count, you simply must let me take charge of your daughters! Neither your family nor I will be here very long this season,

Во втором а́кте бы́ли карти́ны, изобража́ющие монуме́нты и была́ дыра́ в полотне́, изобража́ющая луну́, и абажу́ры на ра́мпе по́дняли, и ста́ли игра́ть в басу́ тру́бы и контраба́сы, и спра́ва и сле́ва вы́шло мно́го люде́й в чёрных ма́нтиях. Лю́ди ста́ли маха́ть рука́ми, и в рука́х у них бы́ло что́-то вро́де кинжа́лов; пото́м прибежа́ли ещё каки́е-то лю́ди и ста́ли тащи́ть прочь ту деви́цу, кото́рая была́ пре́жде в бе́лом, а тепе́рь в голубо́м пла́тье. Они́ не утащи́ли её сра́зу, а до́лго с ней пе́ли, а пото́м уже́ её утащи́ли, и за кули́сами уда́рили три ра́за во что́-то металли́ческое, и все ста́ли на коле́на и запе́ли моли́тву. Не́сколько раз все э́ти де́йствия прерыва́лись восто́рженными кри́ками зри́телей.

Во вре́мя э́того а́кта Ната́ша вся́кий ра́з, как взгля́дывала в парте́р, ви́дела Анато́ля Кура́гина, перекину́вшего ру́ку че́рез спи́нку кре́сла и смотре́вшего на неё. Ей прия́тно бы́ло ви́деть, что он так пленён е́ю, и не приходи́ло в го́лову, что́бы в э́том бы́ло что-нибудь дурно́е.

Когда́ второ́й акт ко́нчился, графи́ня Безу́хова вста́ла, поверну́лась к ло́же Росто́вых (грудь её соверше́нно была́ обнажена́), па́льчиком в перча́тке помани́ла к себе́ ста́рого гра́фа, и не обраща́я внима́ния на воше́дших к ней в ло́жу, начала́ любе́зно улыба́ясь говори́ть с ним.

— Да познако́мьте же меня́ с ва́шими преле́стными дочерьми́, — сказа́ла она́, — весь го́род про них кричи́т, а я их не зна́ю.

Ната́ша вста́ла и присе́ла великоле́пной графи́не. Ната́ше так прия́тна была́ похвала́ э́той блестя́щей краса́вицы, что она́ покрасне́ла от удово́льствия.

— Я тепе́рь то́же хочу́ сде́латься москви́чкой, — говори́ла Эле́н. — И как вам не со́вестно зары́ть таки́е пе́рлы в дере́вне!

Графи́ня Безу́хова, по справедли́вости, име́ла репута́цию обворожи́тельной же́нщины. Она́ могла́ говори́ть то, чего́ не ду́мала, и в осо́бенности льстить, соверше́нно про́сто и нату́рально.

— Нет, ми́лый граф, вы мне позво́льте заня́ться ва́шими дочерьми́. Я хоть тепе́рь здесь не надо́лго. И вы то́же. Я постара́юсь повесели́ть ва́ших. Я ещё в Петербу́рге мно́го слы́шала о вас, и хоте́ла

so I will do what I can to keep them amused. I have already heard so much about you, even in Petersburg, and wanted to get to know you," she said, addressing Natasha with her invariant, perpetually lovely smile. "My page, Drubetskoy, has also spoken of you. Have you heard he is getting married? And so did my husband's friend Bolkonsky, Prince Andrey Bolkonsky," she continued, putting special emphasis on the name, implying that she knew all about his relationship to Natasha. To further their acquaintance, she asked the count to allow one of his daughters to join her in her box for the rest of the performance. So Natasha moved over to sit with her.

In act three the stage was arranged to represent a palace, with a large number of lit candles and pictures of knights with little beards hung on the walls. Two people who were probably supposed to be the king and queen stood in the center. The king waved his right arm and, clearly suffering from stage fright, sang something, but not very well, and then sat down on a crimson throne. The same girl who wore white at the beginning, then had changed into blue, now appeared wearing only a shift. She stood beside the throne with her hair down and mournfully sang something to the queen. But the king waved his arm imperiously and men and women with bare legs came in from both sides of the stage and all of them began dancing as a group. Then the violins played something very light and cheerful while a girl whose bare legs were quite fat, but whose arms were thin, left the others and went into the wings to adjust her bodice. She returned to the center of the stage and began leaping and fluttering her feet together rapidly. Everyone in the theater beat their hands together and shouted "Brava!" When one of the men moved to the corner of the stage, loud cymbals and horns in the orchestra started to play, and this same bare-legged man began to leap very high in the air and mince around on his toes. (This was the dancer, Duport, who was paid sixty thousand rubles a year for doing such things.) All the people in the orchestra, boxes, and balconies began to clap and shout at the top of their lungs; the man stopped what he was doing to smile and bow in all directions. Then a different group of bare-legged men and women danced, and then the king shouted something in time with the music, and

вас узна́ть, – сказа́ла она́ Ната́ше с свое́й однообра́зно-краси́вой улы́бкой. – Я слы́шала о вас и от моего́ пажа́ – Друбецко́го. Вы слы́шали, он же́нится? И от дру́га моего́ му́жа – Болко́нского, кня́зя Андре́я Болко́нского, – сказа́ла она́ с осо́бенным ударе́нием, намека́я э́тим на то, что она́ зна́ла отноше́ния его́ к Ната́ше. – Она́ попроси́ла, чтобы лу́чше познако́миться, позво́лить одно́й из ба́рышень посиде́ть остальну́ю часть спекта́кля в её ло́же, и Ната́ша перешла́ к ней.

В тре́тьем а́кте был на сце́не предста́влен дворе́ц, в кото́ром горе́ло мно́го свече́й и пове́шены бы́ли карти́ны, изобража́вшие ры́царей с боро́дками. В середи́не стоя́ли, вероя́тно, царь и цари́ца. Царь замаха́л пра́вою руко́ю, и, ви́димо робе́я, ду́рно пропе́л что́-то, и сел на мали́новый трон. Деви́ца, бы́вшая снача́ла в бе́лом, пото́м в голубо́м, тепе́рь была́ оде́та в одно́й руба́шке с распу́щенными волоса́ми и стоя́ла о́коло тро́на. Она́ о чём-то го́рестно пе́ла, обраща́ясь к цари́це; но царь стро́го махну́л руко́й, и с боко́в вы́шли мужчи́ны с го́лыми нога́ми и же́нщины с го́лыми нога́ми, и ста́ли танцова́ть все вме́сте. Пото́м скри́пки заигра́ли о́чень то́нко и весело, одна́ из деви́ц с го́лыми то́лстыми нога́ми и худы́ми рука́ми, отдели́вшись от други́х, отошла́ за кули́сы, попра́вила корса́ж, вы́шла на середи́ну и ста́ла пры́гать и ско́ро бить одно́й ного́й о другу́ю. Все в парте́ре захло́пали рука́ми и закрича́ли бра́во. Пото́м оди́н мужчи́на стал в у́гол. В орке́стре заигра́ли гро́мче в цимба́лы и тру́бы, и оди́н э́тот мужчи́на с го́лыми нога́ми стал пры́гать о́чень высоко́ и семени́ть нога́ми. (Мужчи́на э́тот был Duport, получа́вший 60 ты́сяч в год за э́то иску́сство.) Все в парте́ре, в ло́жах и райке́ ста́ли хло́пать и крича́ть и́зо всех сил, и мужчи́на останови́лся и стал улыба́ться и кла́няться на все сто́роны. Пото́м танцова́ли ещё други́е, с го́лыми нога́ми, мужчи́ны и же́нщины, пото́м опя́ть оди́н из царе́й закрича́л что-то под му́зыку, и все ста́ли петь. Но вдруг сде́лалась бу́ря, в орке́стре послы́шались хромати́ческие га́ммы и акко́рды уме́ньшенной

then all of the people on stage sang. Suddenly the orchestra began to play chromatic scales and a diminished seventh, representing a storm, and everyone ran away – again dragging someone or other off into the wings. There was again a great deal of noise and hullabaloo in the theater and everyone began to shout "Duport! Duport! Duport!" Natasha no longer found this strange. She looked around with pleasure, smiling radiantly.

«N'est-ce pas qu'il est admirable?»[5] Hélène asked.

"Oh, oui," Natasha replied.

First published in Russian: 1869
Translation by Lydia Razran Stone

---

5. Isn't he wonderful?

се́птимы, и все побежа́ли и потащи́ли опя́ть одного́ из прису́тствующих за кули́сы, и за́навесь опусти́лась. Опя́ть ме́жду зри́телями подня́лся стра́шный шум и треск, и все с восто́рженными ли́цами ста́ли крича́ть: Дюпо́ра! Дюпо́ра! Дюпо́ра! Ната́ша уже́ не находи́ла э́того стра́нным. Она́ с удово́льствием, ра́достно улыба́ясь, смотре́ла вокру́г себя́.

– *N'est ce pas qu'il est admirable – Duport?* – сказа́ла Эле́н, обраща́ясь к ней.

– *Oh, oui,* – отвеча́ла Ната́ша.

This excerpt from *War and Peace* depicts the battle experience of 16-year-old Petya Rostov at the tail end of Napoleon's Russian campaign, precisely 200 years ago this year. Here we see Tolstoy's view of war as chaos, in which each individual acts for himself on the basis of impulse and yet no one is in control of his own fate. In this short pair of chapters, Tolstoy provides a stunning depiction of the glamor of the myth of war to an impressionable adolescent, and this excerpt contains one of Tolstoy's most brilliant descriptions of transcendent human experiences. Unlike the extremely simple rendering of Olenin's reaction to the mountains in *The Cossacks*, Petya's fugue is described with stunning verbal pyrotechnics.

Petya's Fugue

War and Peace
Volume IV, Part III

X

Petya arrived at the watchman's hut to find Denisov standing at the door. Denisov had been waiting for Petya's return in a state of anxious agitation, angry at himself for having permitted the boy to go.

"Thank God! Oh, thank God!" he repeated, as he listened to Petya's rapturous account of his adventure. "But, the Devil take you! I haven't slept a wink fretting about you![1] Well, thank God, you're here! Now go to bed; there's still a little time to sleep before morning."

"No, really. I'm not ready to go to sleep yet. Besides, I know how I am, if I go to sleep now, no one will be able to wake me in the morning. And I never like to sleep the night before a battle."

Petya sat for a while in the hut reviewing, and relishing, the details of the mission he had just completed, while vividly imagining what would

---

1. Tolstoy gives the character Denisov a speech defect in which he pronounces a guttural French "r" instead of the normal Russian one and portrays this in each of his speeches. We have found no way to portray this defect without making Densisov appear cartoonish and/or distracting attention from the story

Пе́тина му́зика

Война́ и мир
Том IV, Часть III

X

Верну́вшись к карау́лке, Пе́тя заста́л Дени́сова в сеня́х. Дени́сов в волне́нии, беспоко́йстве и доса́де на себя́, что отпусти́л Пе́тю, ожида́л его́.

– Сла́ва бо́гу! – кри́кнул он. – Ну, Сла́ва Бо́гу! – повторя́л он, слу́шая восто́рженный расска́з Пе́ти. – И чег'т тебя́ возьми́, из-за тебя́ не спал! – проговори́л Дени́сов. Ну, сла́ва бо́гу, тепе́рь ложи́сь спать. Ещё вздремнём до у́тра.

– Да... Нет, – сказа́л Пе́тя. – Мне ещё не хо́чется спать. Да я и себя́ зна́ю, е́жели засну́, так уж ко́нчено. И пото́м я привы́к не спать пе́ред сраже́нием.

Пе́тя посиде́л не́сколько вре́мени в избе́, ра́достно вспомина́я подро́бности свое́й пое́здки и жи́во представля́я себе́ то, что бу́дет

happen the next day. When he noticed that Denisov had fallen asleep, he got up and went outside.

It was still completely dark. The rain had passed, but drops still fell from the trees. He could barely make out the black shapes near the watchman's hut – Cossacks' straw shelters, and horses tethered together. Behind the hut were more black shapes: two wagons with horses beside them. The dying campfire glowed red in the hollow. Some of the Cossacks and hussars were awake. He heard soft voices; their whispering mingling with the sounds of trees dripping and horses munching.

Petya left the hut, peered into the darkness, then walked over to the wagons. The sound of snoring came from beneath one of them. Saddled horses stood about, munching on oats. Even in the dark, Petya recognized his own horse, to whom he had given the Caucasian name Karabakh, although he was actually bred in Ukraine. He went over to him.

"Well, Karabakh! We have a big job to do tomorrow!" he said, rubbing his face against his muzzle and giving him a kiss.

"Can't you sleep, sir?" said a Cossack sitting under one of the wagons.

"No, ah… Likhachyov, that's your name, isn't it? Do you know I have only just gotten back! We managed to sneak into the French camp."

And Petya proceeded to give the Cossack a detailed account of his foray and the reason for it. He concluded by explaining to him why it was better to risk one's life for a purpose than to act without a conscious plan.

"All the same," said the Cossack, "you'd be better off going to sleep now."

"No, no, I'm used to this," said Petya. "But tell me, maybe the flints in your pistols are worn out? I have some with me. Can you use them? Please, take what you need."

The Cossack poked his head out from under the wagon to take a closer look at Petya.

"I'm used to planning ahead, you know," said Petya. "Some people just do whatever seems easiest at the time, with no preparation, but they end up regretting it. That's not the way I like to do things."

зáвтра. Потóм, замéтив, что Денúсов заснýл, он встал и пошёл на двор.

На дворé ещё бы́ло совсéм темнó. Дóждик прошёл, но кáпли ещё пáдали с дерéвьев. Вблизú от караýлки виднéлись чёрные фигýры казáчьих шалашéй и свя́занных вмéсте лошадéй. За избýшкой чернéлись две фýры, у котóрых стоя́ли лóшади, и в оврáге краснéлся догорáвший огóнь. Казáки и гусáры не все спáли: кое-гдé слы́шались, вмéсте с звýком пáдающих кáпель и блúзкого звýка жевáния лошадéй, негрóмкие, как бы шéпчущиеся голосá.

Пéтя вы́шел из сéней, оглядéлся в темнотé и подошёл к фýрам. Под фýрами храпéл ктó-то, и вокрýг них стоя́ли, жуя́ овёс, осéдланные лóшади. В темнотé Пéтя узнáл свою́ лóшадь, котóрую он называл Карабáхом, хотя́ онá былá малороссúйская лóшадь, и подошёл к ней.

— Ну, Карабáх, зáвтра послýжим, — сказáл он, ню́хая её нóздри и целýя её.

— Что, бáрин, не спúте? — сказáл казáк, сидéвший под фýрой.

— Нет; а... Лихачёв, кáжется, тебя́ звать? Ведь я сейчáс тóлько приéхал. Мы éздили к францýзам. —И Пéтя подрóбно рассказáл казакý не тóлько свою́ поéздку, но и то, почемý он éздил и почемý он считáет, что лýчше рисковáть своéй жúзнью, чем дéлать наобýм Лáзаря.

— Чтó же, соснýли бы, — сказáл казáк.

— Нет, я привы́к, — отвечáл Пéтя. — А что, у вас кремнú в пистолéтах не обúлись? Я привёз с собóю. Не нýжно ли? Ты возьмú.

Казáк вы́сунулся из-пóд фýры, чтóбы поблúже рассмотрéть Пéтю.

— Оттогó, что я привы́к всё дéлать аккурáтно, — сказáл Пéтя. — Ины́е так, коé-как, не приготóвятся, потóм и жалéют. Я так не люблю́.

"You know best," said the Cossack.

"Oh yes, another thing! Would you please do me a favor and sharpen my saber for me?" Petya started to say that his saber was blunt from use, but couldn't bring himself to lie and ended up admitting that it had not yet been sharpened. "Do you think you could do that?"

"Sure I could."

Likhachyov got up and rummaged in his pack. Soon Petya heard the battlefield sound of steel on whetstone. He climbed up and sat on the edge of the wagon while the Cossack remained underneath it, sharpening the saber.

"Are the men asleep?" Petya asked.

"Some are asleep and some are awake – like us."

"What about the French boy?"[2]

"Vesenny? Oh, he's dead to the world in that pile of hay. He was out like a light, exhausted after being so scared. He couldn't wait!"

Petya said nothing for a long time after that exchange, listening to the sounds around him. Then he heard footsteps and a black figure emerged from the dark.

"What are you sharpening?" asked the man, approaching the wagon.

"Why, this gentleman's saber."

"Very good," said the man, whom Petya took to be a hussar. "Was there a cup left lying around here?"

"Over there, by the wheel!"

The hussar took the cup.

"It should be getting light soon," he yawned and walked off.

Petya must have realized at some level that he was in the woods with Denisov's guerrillas, sitting on a captured French wagon with horses tethered to it, less than a mile from the road. A Cossack called Likhachyov was under the wagon, sharpening his saber for him. The large black shape to his right was the watchman's hut, the red glow down to the left was the

2. The reference is to Vincent, a young French drummer boy who had been taken into the regiment as a half prisoner-half mascot instead of sending him with the adult prisoners of war.

— Это то́чно, – сказа́л каза́к.

— Да ещё во́т что, пожа́луйста, голу́бчик, наточи́ мне са́блю; затупи́... (но Пе́тя боя́лся солга́ть) она́ никогда́ отто́чена не была́. Мо́жно э́то сде́лать?

— Отчего́ ж, мо́жно.

Лихачёв встал, поры́лся в вью́ках, и Пе́тя ско́ро услыха́л во́инственный звук ста́ли о брусо́к. Он влез на фу́ру и сел на край её. Каза́к под фу́рой точи́л са́блю.

— А что́ же, спят молодцы́? – сказа́л Пе́тя.

— Кто спит, а кто так во́т.

— Ну, а ма́льчик что?

— Весе́нний-то? Он там, в сенца́х, завали́лся. Со стра́ху спи́тся. Уж рад-то был.

До́лго по́сле э́того Пе́тя молча́л, прислу́шиваясь к зву́кам. В темноте́ послы́шались шаги́ и показа́лась чёрная фигу́ра.

— Что то́чишь? – спроси́л челове́к, подходя́ к фу́ре.

— А во́т ба́рину наточи́ть са́блю.

— Хоро́шее де́ло, – сказа́л челове́к, кото́рый показа́лся Пе́те гуса́ром. –У вас, что́ ли, ча́шка оста́лась?

— А вон у колеса́.

Гуса́р взял ча́шку.

— Небо́сь ско́ро свет, – проговори́л он, зева́я, и прошёл куда́-то.

Пе́тя до́лжен бы был знать, что он в лесу́, в па́ртии Дени́сова, в версте́ от доро́ги, что он сиди́т на фу́ре, отби́той у францу́зов, о́коло кото́рой привя́заны ло́шади, что под ним сиди́т каза́к Лихачёв и ната́чивает ему́ са́блю, что большо́е чёрное пятно́ напра́во – карау́лка, и кра́сное я́ркое пятно́

dying campfire, and the man looking for his cup was a hussar who wanted a drink of water. But Petya was neither conscious of this, nor did he want to know anything about it. He was in a magical realm, where nothing resembled real life. The big dark shape could be the watchman's hut, but it could just as easily be an underground passage leading to the depths of the earth. That red glow might come from a campfire, but it might also be the eye of a gigantic monster. Maybe he really was sitting on a wagon, but it was just as likely that he was instead perched on top of an incredibly high tower, from which, if he happened to fall, it might take a day, or a month, or even forever to reach the ground. Maybe there was simply a friendly Cossack named Likhachyov sitting under the wagon; but mightn't this fellow also be the kindest, bravest, most wonderful and splendid man in the world, whose remarkable qualities no one had yet recognized? Maybe the hussar who had come for water had simply gone back to the camp in the hollow; or maybe, when he disappeared from view, he simply vanished off the face of the earth and no longer existed at all.

Nothing that Petya might have seen now would have surprised him. He was in the realm of fantasy, where absolutely anything was possible.

He looked up at the sky. And, like the earth, the sky was a magical realm. It had cleared; clouds scudded over treetops as if a curtain was being drawn to reveal the stars. Sometimes it looked as if the clouds were passing off, leaving patches of clear black sky; but then the black areas appeared to be the clouds. Sometimes the sky seemed to stretch infinitely high overhead, and then it appeared to descend so low that you could reach up and touch it with your hand.

Petya's eyelids drooped, he almost toppled over.

Trees were dripping. People spoke softly. Horses neighed and jostled each other. Someone was snoring.

"Ozheeg-zheeg, Ozheeg-zheeg." the saber hissed against the whetstone. Suddenly Petya seemed to hear a marvelous orchestra play something he did not recognize, a solemn, lovely hymn. Petya was as naturally musical as Natasha, more so than Nikolai. But because he had never studied music

внизу́ нале́во – догора́вший костёр, что челове́к, приходи́вший за ча́шкой, – гуса́р, кото́рый хоте́л пить; но он ничего́ не знал и не хоте́л знать э́того. Он был в волше́бном ца́рстве, в кото́ром ничего́ не́ было похо́жего на действи́тельность. Большо́е чёрное пятно́, мо́жет быть, то́чно была́ карау́лка, а мо́жет быть, была́ пеще́ра, кото́рая вела́ в са́мую глубь земли́. Кра́сное пятно́, мо́жет быть, был огóнь, а мо́жет быть – глаз огро́много чудо́вища. Мо́жет быть, он то́чно сиди́т тепе́рь на фу́ре, а о́чень мо́жет быть, что он сиди́т не на фу́ре, а на стра́шно высо́кой ба́шне, с кото́рой е́жели упа́сть, то лете́ть бы до земли́ це́лый день, це́лый ме́сяц – всё лете́ть и никогда́ не долети́шь. Мо́жет быть, что под фу́рой сиди́т про́сто каза́к Лихачёв, а о́чень мо́жет быть, что э́то – са́мый до́брый, хра́брый, са́мый чуде́сный, са́мый превосхо́дный челове́к на све́те, кото́рого никто́ не зна́ет. Мо́жет быть, э́то то́чно проходи́л гуса́р за водо́й и пошёл в лощи́ну, а мо́жет быть, он то́лько что исче́з из ви́ду и совсе́м исче́з, и его́ не́ было.

Что́ бы ни увида́л тепе́рь Пе́тя, ничто́ бы не удиви́ло его́. Он был в волше́бном ца́рстве, в кото́ром всё бы́ло возмо́жно.

Он погляде́л на не́бо. И не́бо бы́ло тако́е же волше́бное, как и земля́. На не́бе расчища́ло, и над верши́нами дере́в бы́стро бежа́ли облака́, как бу́дто открыва́я звёзды. Иногда́ каза́лось, что на не́бе расчища́ло и пока́зывалось чёрное, чи́стое не́бо. Иногда́ каза́лось, что э́ти чёрные пя́тна бы́ли ту́чки. Иногда́ каза́лось, что не́бо высоко́, высоко́ поднима́ется над голово́й; иногда́ не́бо спуска́лось совсе́м, та́к что руко́й мо́жно бы́ло доста́ть его́.

Пе́тя стал закрыва́ть глаза́ и пока́чиваться.

Ка́пли ка́пали. Шёл ти́хий го́вор. Ло́шади заржа́ли и подрали́сь. Храпе́л кто́-то.

– Ожи́г, жиг, ожи́г, жиг... – свисте́ла ната́чиваемая са́бля. И вдруг Пе́тя услыха́л стро́йный хор му́зыки, игра́вшей како́й-то неизве́стный, торже́ственно сла́дкий гимн. Пе́тя был музыка́лен, та́к же как

or even thought much about it, the musical themes that entered his mind unexpectedly struck him as especially original and enchanting. The music swelled. The theme developed and passed from one instrument to another. It was what musicians call a fugue, although Petya did not know the first thing about fugues. Two instruments – one something like a violin and the other like a trumpet, but with a more beautiful and purer sound than either – picked up the theme. Each played its own part, but before the theme came to an end, they played a nearly, but not quite identical, theme together. Then a third and fourth instrument joined in and they merged and played together, then separated into parts, then merged again, by turns solemn and religious, then brilliant and triumphant.

"I must have dreamed it!!" Petya said to himself as he woke with a start. "It was all in my head… Maybe this was my own composition – my own music. One more time, please. Play on, Petya's music, play on! Yes, like that!"

As he closed his eyes, the sounds seemed to come from a distance and surround him. These wonderful notes trembled, blended into harmonies, separated, blended again, and then merged into the same solemn and lovely hymn as before. "Oh, this is wonderful! It will play as much as I like and however I like!" Petya told himself, as in his mind he again attempted to direct his enormous orchestra.

"Now die away, softly, softly!" and the music obeyed him. "Now fuller, more joyful. Louder and more lively now. Now, more and more joyful!" A crescendo of triumphant sounds rose from a deep unknown source. "Chorus, join in now!" Petya commanded. And he heard men's voices first, then women's voices approaching from a great distance. The voices swelled in a powerful crescendo of triumphant harmony and the surpassing beauty transfixed Petya with awe and joy.

The voices blended into the instruments' solemn victory march, the sound of dripping, and the vzheeg, zheeg, zheeg of the saber, and when the horses jostled and neighed, the sounds, instead of interrupting the music, enhanced it.

Ната́ша, и бо́льше Никола́я, но он никогда́ не учи́лся му́зыке, не ду́мал о му́зыке, и потому́ моти́вы, неожи́данно приходи́вшие ему́ в го́лову, бы́ли для него́ осо́бенно но́вы и привлека́тельны. Му́зыка игра́ла всё слышне́е и слышне́е. Напе́в разраста́лся, переходи́л из одного́ инструме́нта в друго́й. Происходи́ло то, что называ́ется фу́гой, хотя́ Пе́тя не име́л ни мале́йшего поня́тия о том, что тако́е фу́га. Ка́ждый инструме́нт, то похо́жий на скри́пку, то на тру́бы — но лу́чше и чи́ще, чем скри́пки и тру́бы, — ка́ждый инструме́нт игра́л своё и, не доигра́в ещё моти́ва, слива́лся с други́м, начина́вшим почти́ то же, и с тре́тьим, и с четвёртым, и все они́ слива́лись в одно́ и опя́ть разбега́лись, и опя́ть слива́лись то в торже́ственно церко́вное, то в я́рко блестя́щее и побе́дное.

«Ах, да, ведь э́то я во сне, — качну́вшись наперёд, сказа́л себе́ Пе́тя. —Это у меня́ в уша́х. А мо́жет быть, э́то моя́ му́зыка. Ну, опя́ть. Валя́й моя́ му́зыка! Ну!..»

Он закры́л глаза́. И с ра́зных сторо́н, как бу́дто издалека́, затрепета́ли зву́ки, ста́ли сла́живаться, разбега́ться, слива́ться, и опя́ть всё соедини́лось в тот же сла́дкий и торже́ственный гимн. «Ах, э́то пре́лесть что тако́е! Ско́лько хочу́ и как хочу́», — сказа́л себе́ Пе́тя. Он попро́бовал руководи́ть э́тим огро́мным хо́ром инструме́нтов.

«Ну, ти́ше, ти́ше, замира́йте тепе́рь. —И зву́ки слу́шались его́. —Ну, тепе́рь полне́е, веселе́е. Ещё, ещё ра́достнее. —И из неизве́стной глубины́ поднима́лись уси́ливающиеся, торже́ственные зву́ки. —Ну, голоса́, пристава́йте!» — приказа́л Пе́тя. И снача́ла издалека́ послы́шались голоса́ мужски́е, пото́м же́нские. Голоса́ росли́, росли́ в равноме́рном торже́ственном уси́лии. Пе́те стра́шно и ра́достно бы́ло внима́ть их необыча́йной красоте́.

С торже́ственным побе́дным ма́ршем слива́лась пе́сня, и ка́пли ка́пали, и вжиг, жиг, жиг... свисте́ла са́бля, и опя́ть подрали́сь и заржа́ли ло́шади, не наруша́я хо́ра, а входя́ в него́.

Petya had no idea how long all this went on; he reveled in it; astonished at his own delight, he was sorry he had no one with whom to share it. He was roused, finally, as Likhachyov's friendly voice said, "All ready, your honor; now you'll be able to split a Frenchman right in half with it!"

Petya woke up.

"It's getting light, it's finally getting light!" he exclaimed.

As a watery light glimmered through bare branches, what before appeared merely as shapes in the darkness were now visible as horses, complete with tails. Petya shook himself, jumped up, took a ruble from his pocket and gave it to Likhachyov. He swirled his saber up, down, and around, tested its edge, then thrust it into his scabbard. The Cossacks, meanwhile, untethered their horses and tightened the saddle girths.

"Here comes the commander," Likhachyov said.

As Denisov emerged from the watchman's hut, he called out to Petya and ordered the men to get ready.

XI

Working in half-darkness, the men quickly found their horses, tightened the girths and formed themselves into companies. Denisov stood near the watchman's hut to give final instructions. The infantry marched down the road in the predawn mist; hundreds of feet slogged through the mud, and soon disappeared among the trees. The *yesaul*[3] gave more orders to the Cossacks. Petya held his horse by the bridle, waiting impatiently for the order to mount. He had just splashed his face with cold water, so it glowed and there was fire in his eyes. Cold shivers ran down his spine and his whole body trembled.

"Well, is everything ready?" asked Denisov. "Bring the horses."

The horses were brought. Denisov shouted angrily at the Cossack that the saddle girths were too slack, and then he mounted. Petya put his foot in the stirrup. As usual, his horse tried to nip him in the leg, but Petya was

----

3. The yesaul was the aide de camp of the hetman, the Cossack chief.

Пётя не знал, как до́лго э́то продолжа́лось: он наслажда́лся, всё время удивля́лся своему́ наслажде́нию и жале́л, что не́кому сообщи́ть его́. Его́ разбуди́л ла́сковый го́лос Лихачёва.

— Гото́во, ва́ше благоро́дие, на́двое хранцу́за распласта́ете.

Пётя очну́лся.

— Уж света́ет, пра́во, света́ет! — вскри́кнул он.

Неви́дные пре́жде ло́шади ста́ли видны́ до хвосто́в, и сквозь оголённые ве́тки видне́лся водяни́стый свет. Пётя встряхну́лся, вскочи́л, доста́л из карма́на целко́вый и дал Лихачёву, махну́в, попро́бовал ша́шку и положи́л её в ножны́. Каза́ки отвя́зывали лошаде́й и подтя́гивали подпру́ги.

Вот и команди́р, — сказа́л Лихачёв. Из карау́лки вы́шел Дени́сов и, окли́кнув Пётю, приказа́л собира́ться.

XI

Бы́стро в полутьме́ разобра́ли лошаде́й, подтяну́ли подпру́ги и разобра́лись по кома́ндам. Дени́сов стоя́л у карау́лки, отдава́я после́дние приказа́ния. Пехо́та па́ртии, шлёпая со́тней ног, прошла́ вперёд по доро́ге и бы́стро скры́лась ме́жду дере́вьев в предрассве́тном тума́не. Эсау́л что́-то прика́зывал каза́кам. Пётя держа́л свою́ ло́шадь в поводу́, с нетерпе́нием ожида́я приказа́ния сади́ться. Обмы́тое холо́дной водо́й, лицо́ его́, в осо́бенности глаза́ горе́ли огнём, озно́б пробега́л по спине́, и во всём те́ле что́-то бы́стро и равноме́рно дрожа́ло.

— Ну, гото́во у вас всё? — сказа́л Дени́сов. —Дава́й лошаде́й.

Лошаде́й по́дали. Дени́сов рассерди́лся на каза́ка за то, что подпру́ги бы́ли слабы́, и, разбрани́в его́, сел. Пётя взя́лся за

too quick for him. He leaped into the saddle as if weightless. After turning around to look at the hussars moving behind him in the darkness, he rode up to Denisov.

"Vasily Fyodorovich," he called out, "for the love of God, give me an assignment! Please!"

Denisov seemed to have forgotten Petya's very existence. He turned to glance at him.

"I ask only one thing of you," he admonished, "do what I tell you and refrain from purposely putting yourself anywhere in the path of danger."

He rode in silence the whole way without saying another word to Petya. It was appreciably lighter when they reached the edge of the forest. After Denisov whispered something to the *yesaul*, the Cossacks overtook him and Petya. After all of them had passed, Denisov spurred his horse and rode down the hill. The horses slipped in the mud and slid on their haunches as their riders headed into the ravine. Petya rode beside Denisov, trembling more and more. It grew lighter and lighter, although objects at any distance were still obscured by the mist. Denisov looked back when they reached the bottom and nodded to the Cossack who stood beside him.

"Give the signal!" he said.

The Cossack raised his arm and a shot rang out. The sound of hoofbeats followed instantaneously, then shouting from all sides and more shots.

Petya lashed his horse as the hoofbeats and shouting began, loosening his reins and ignoring Denisov's shouts, he galloped ahead. At the exact moment the shots rang out, it seemed to Petya that it was suddenly as bright as noon. He galloped toward the bridge, following the Cossacks ahead of him along the road. He almost collided with a Cossack who had fallen behind on the bridge, but passed him. Some people in front of him, undoubtedly Frenchmen, ran across the road from right to left. One of them fell in the mud right under Petya's horse's hooves.

стре́мя. Ло́шадь, по привы́чке, хоте́ла кусну́ть его́ за но́гу, но Пе́тя, не чу́вствуя свое́й тя́жести, бы́стро вскочи́л в седло́ и, огля́дываясь на тро́нувшихся сза́ди в темноте́ гуса́р, подъе́хал к Дени́сову.

— Васи́лий Фёдорович, вы мне пору́чите что-нибудь? Пожа́луйста... ра́ди Бо́га... — сказа́л он. Дени́сов, каза́лось, забы́л про существова́ние Пе́ти. Он огляну́лся на него́.

— Об одно́м тебя́ пг'ошу́, — сказа́л он стро́го, — слу́шаться меня́ и никуда́ не сова́ться.

Во всё вре́мя перее́зда Дени́сов ни сло́ва не говори́л бо́льше с Пе́тей и е́хал мо́лча. Когда́ подъе́хали к опу́шке ле́са, в по́ле заме́тно уже́ ста́ло светле́ть. Дени́сов поговори́л что́-то шёпотом с эсау́лом, и каза́ки ста́ли проезжа́ть ми́мо Пе́ти и Дени́сова. Когда́ они́ все прое́-хали, Дени́сов тро́нул свою́ ло́шадь и пое́хал под го́ру. Садя́сь на зады́ и скользя́, ло́шади спуска́лись с свои́ми седока́ми в лощи́ну. Пе́тя е́хал ря́дом с Дени́совым. Дрожь во всём его́ те́ле всё уси́ливалась. Ста-нови́лось всё светле́е и светле́е, то́лько тума́н скрыва́л отдалённые предме́ты. Съе́хав вниз и огляну́вшись наза́д, Дени́сов кивну́л голо-во́й казаку́, стоя́вшему по́дле него́.

— Сигна́л! — проговори́л он.

Каза́к по́днял ру́ку, разда́лся вы́стрел. И в то же мгнове́ние послы́-шался то́пот впереди́ поскака́вших лошаде́й, кри́ки с ра́зных сторо́н и ещё вы́стрелы.

В то же мгнове́ние, как раздали́сь пе́рвые зву́ки то́пота и кри́ка, Пе́тя, уда́рив свою́ ло́шадь и вы́пустив пово́дья, не слу́шая Дени́сова, крича́вшего на него́, поскака́л вперёд. Пе́те показа́лось, что вдруг со-верше́нно, как се́редь дня, я́рко рассвело́ в ту мину́ту, как послы́шался вы́стрел. Он подскака́л к мосту́. Впереди́ по доро́ге скака́ли каза́ки. На мосту́ он столкну́лся с отста́вшим каза́ком и поскака́л да́льше. Впе-реди́ каки́е-то лю́ди, — должно́ быть, э́то бы́ли францу́зы, — бежа́ли с пра́вой стороны́ доро́ги на ле́вую. Оди́н упа́л в грязь под нога́ми Пе́тиной ло́шади.

A group of Cossacks surrounded a hut, intent on something. Horrible screams came from the midst of the crowd. Petya galloped up to see a Frenchman, with pale face and trembling jaw, clutching the handle of a lance aimed at him.

"Hurrah!" Petya shouted, "Come on men, victory is ours!!" Giving rein to his agitated horse, he galloped onward into the village street.

He heard shooting ahead. Cossacks, hussars, and ragged Russian prisoners, who came running from both sides of the road, shouted loudly and incoherently. A dashing-looking, bareheaded Frenchman wearing a blue overcoat, with a scowl on his red face, was defending himself against the hussars with his bayonet. The Frenchman was already down when Petya galloped up. "I'm too late again!" flashed through Petya's mind, and he galloped onward to the spot where he heard rapid gunfire. The firing came from the yard of the manor house where he and Dolokhov had been the night before. The French were making a stand behind a wattle fence of an overgrown garden, shooting at the Cossacks who crowded around the gate. Petya caught sight of Dolokhov through the smoke as he approached the gate. Dolokhov's face was pale, greenish, as he shouted to his men. "Go round the back! Wait for the infantry!" he yelled as Petya rode up.

"Why wait? Hurraaah!" shouted Petya. Without hesitating for an instant, he galloped toward the source of the firing, where the smoke was thickest.

There was a volley of gunfire; some bullets whistled past without hitting anything, while others could be heard smacking into something. Dolokhov and the Cossacks galloped through the gate behind Petya. Some of the French threw down their arms in the dense wavering smoke and ran out of the bushes to meet the Cossacks; others ran down the hill toward a pond. Petya could be seen galloping through the courtyard, spasmodically waving both his arms instead of holding the reins and slipping further and further to one side of his saddle. As his horse galloped up to a smoldering campfire and stopped suddenly, Petya fell heavily to the wet ground. The

У одно́й избы́ столпи́лись каза́ки, что́-то де́лая. Из середи́ны толпы́ послы́шался стра́шный крик. Пе́тя подскака́л к э́той толпе́, и пе́рвое, что он увида́л, бы́ло бле́дное, с трясу́щейся ни́жней че́люстью лицо́ францу́за, держа́вшегося за дре́вко напра́вленной на него́ пи́ки.

— Ура́!.. Ребя́та... на́ши... — прокрича́л Пе́тя и, дав пово́дья разгоря́чи́вшейся ло́шади, поскака́л вперёд по у́лице.

Впереди́ слышны́ бы́ли вы́стрелы. Каза́ки, гуса́ры и ру́сские обо́рванные пле́нные, бежа́вшие с обе́их сторо́н доро́ги, все гро́мко и нескла́дно крича́ли что́-то. Молодцева́тый, без ша́пки, с кра́сным нахму́ренным лицо́м, францу́з в си́ней шине́ли отбива́лся штыко́м от гуса́ров. Когда́ Пе́тя подскака́л, францу́з уже́ упа́л. Опя́ть опозда́л, мелькну́ло в голове́ Пе́ти, и он поскака́л туда́, отку́да слы́шались ча́стые вы́стрелы. Вы́стрелы раздава́лись на дворе́ того́ ба́рского до́ма, на кото́ром он был вчера́ но́чью с До́лоховым. Францу́зы засе́ли там за плетнём в густо́м, заро́сшем куста́ми саду́ и стреля́ли по каза́кам, столпи́вшимся у воро́т. Подъезжа́я к воро́там, Пе́тя в порохово́м дыму́ увида́л До́лохова с бле́дным, зеленова́тым лицо́м, крича́вшего что́-то лю́дям. «В объе́зд! Пехо́ту подожда́ть!» — крича́л он, в то вре́мя как Пе́тя подъе́хал к нему́.

— Подожда́ть?.. Ура́аааа!.. — закрича́л Пе́тя и, не ме́для ни одно́й мину́ты, поскака́л к тому́ ме́сту, отку́да слы́шались вы́стрелы и где гу́ще был порохово́й дым.

Послы́шался залп, провизжа́ли пусты́е и во что-то шлёпнувшие пу́ли. Каза́ки и До́лохов скака́ли всле́д за Пе́тей в воро́та до́ма. Францу́зы в коле́блющемся густо́м ды́ме одни́ броса́ли ору́жие и выбега́ли из кусто́в навстре́чу каза́кам, други́е бежа́ли под го́ру к пруду́. Пе́тя скака́л на свое́й ло́шади вдоль по ба́рскому двору́ и, вме́сто того́ чтобы держа́ть пово́дья, стра́нно и бы́стро маха́л обе́ими рука́ми и всё да́льше и да́льше сбива́лся с седла́ на одну́ сто́рону. Ло́шадь, набежа́в на тле́вший в у́треннем све́те костёр, упёрлась, и Пе́тя тяжело́ упа́л на мо́крую зе́млю. Каза́ки ви́дели,

Cossacks watched his arms and legs jerk rapidly, while his head remained still. A bullet had pierced his skull.

After he spoke to the senior French officer, who came out of the house with a white handkerchief tied to his sword as a sign of surrender, Dolokhov dismounted and went to Petya, who lay motionless with arms outstretched.

"Done for!" he said with a frown, and went to the gate to meet Denisov, who rode toward him.

"Dead?" cried Denisov, who could recognize from a distance the all too familiar lifeless aspect of Petya's body.

"Done for!" repeated Dolokhov, as if he took pleasure in saying those words. He approached the captured French prisoners quickly, as the Cossacks rushed to surround them. "We won't be taking these guys with us!" he called out to Denisov.

Denisov did not reply. He dismounted by Petya's body and, with trembling hands, turned over the bloodstained, mud-spattered face, which had already turned white.

He recalled Petya's words, "I am used to having something sweet to eat. These are fine raisins, have some, take them all!" The Cossacks looked around in surprise as Denisov made a sound like the howl of a dog. Then he turned away, walked over to the wattle fence, and held onto it for support.

Among the Russian prisoners Denisov and Dolokhov rescued was Pierre Bezukhov.

First published in Russian: 1869
Translation by Lydia Razran Stone

как бы́стро задёргались его́ ру́ки и но́ги, несмотря́ на то, что голова́ его́ не шевели́лась. Пу́ля проби́ла ему́ го́лову.

Переговори́вши с ста́ршим францу́зским офице́ром, кото́рый вы́шел к нему́ из-за до́ма с платко́м на шпа́ге и объяви́л, что они́ сда-ю́тся, До́лохов слез с ло́шади и подошёл к неподви́жно, с раски́ну-тыми рука́ми, лежа́вшему Пе́те.

— Гото́в, — сказа́л он, нахму́рившись, и пошёл в воро́та навстре́чу е́хавшему к нему́ Дени́сову.

— Уби́т?! — вскри́кнул Дени́сов, увида́в ещё издалека́ то знако́мое ему́, несомне́нно безжи́зненное положе́ние, в кото́ром лежа́ло те́ло Пе́ти.

— Гото́в, — повтори́л До́лохов, как бу́дто выгова́ривание э́того сло́ва доставля́ло ему́ удово́льствие, и бы́стро пошёл к пле́нным, кото́рых окружи́ли спе́шившиеся каза́ки. -Брать не бу́дем! - кри́кнул он Дени́сову.

Дени́сов не отвеча́л; он подъе́хал к Пе́те, слез с ло́шади и дрожа́-щими рука́ми поверну́л к себе́ запа́чканное кро́вью и гря́зью, уже́ побледне́вшее лицо́ Пе́ти.

«Я привы́к что́-нибудь сла́дкое. Отли́чный изю́м, бери́те весь», — вспо́мнилось ему́. И каза́ки с удивле́нием огляну́лись на зву́ки, похо́жие на соба́чий лай, с кото́рыми Дени́сов бы́стро отверну́лся, подошёл к плетню́ и схвати́лся за него́.

В числе́ отби́тых Дени́совым и До́лоховым ру́сских пле́нных был Пьер Безу́хов.

Lev Nikolaevich Tolstoy
Ilya Repin (1887)

There have been so many translations of Tolstoy's great works, yet rarely does anyone (except professional translators) consider the differences or merits of different translations. So editor Lydia Razran Stone selected a special passage from *Anna Karenina* and analyzed some of its translations.

Levin's Epiphany
Lydia Razran Stone

The passage below was chosen because it is so important both to the themes of the novel and to Tolstoy's evolving philosophy.

Tolstoy's major works usually contain alter egos, and with the exception of Olenin (in *The Cossacks*), who seems very like Tolstoy's egocentric, dissolute, but good natured and sensitive younger self, none are featured in the excerpts in this volume. Levin (one of the main characters in *Anna Karenina*) is Tolstoy's alter ego *par excellence,* and the philosophy that saves him from his depression at the seeming meaninglessness of life in the face of death is identical in function, as well as similar in content, to Tolstoy's. The passage was not chosen to specifically highlight differences in translations; some other selection might have served that purpose better, yet this passage might also therefore be seen as more normative for all the translations.

On the translations: There appear to be three periods during which new English translations of *Anna Karenina* were published: 1886-1918;

1954-1961 and 2000-2008. Six translations were found and examined. Three are discussed here, one to represent each period.

Original Passage

Фёдор говори́т, что Кири́ллов, дво́рник, живёт для брю́ха. Э́то поня́тно и разу́мно. Мы все, как разу́мные существа́, не мо́жем ина́че жить, как для брю́ха. И вдруг тот же Фёдор говори́т, что для брю́ха жить ду́рно, а на́до жить для пра́вды, для Бо́га, и я с намёка понима́ю его́! И я и миллио́ны люде́й, жи́вших века́ тому́ наза́д и живу́щих тепе́рь, мужики́, ни́щие ду́хом и мудрецы́, ду́мавшие и писа́вшие об э́том, свои́м нея́сным языко́м говоря́щие то же, – мы все согла́сны в э́том одно́м: для чего́ на́до жить и что́ хорошо́. Я со все́ми людьми́ име́ю то́лько одно́ твёрдое, несомне́нное и я́сное зна́ние, и зна́ние э́то не мо́жет быть объяснено́ ра́зумом – оно́ вне его́ и не име́ет никаки́х причи́н и не мо́жет име́ть никаки́х после́дствий.

Е́сли добро́ име́ет причи́ну, оно́ уже́ не добро́; е́сли оно́ име́ет после́дствие – награ́ду, оно́ то́же не добро́. Ста́ло быть, добро́ вне цепи́ причи́н и сле́дствий.

И его́-то я зна́ю, и все мы зна́ем.

А я иска́л чуде́с, жале́л, что не вида́л чу́да, кото́рое бы убеди́ло меня́. А вот оно́ чу́до, еди́нственно возмо́жное, постоя́нно существу́ющее, со всех сторо́н окружа́ющее меня́, и я не замеча́л его́!

Како́е же мо́жет быть чу́до бо́льше э́того?

Неуже́ли я нашёл разреше́ние всего́, неуже́ли ко́нчены тепе́рь мои́ страда́ния? – ду́мал Ле́вин, шага́я по пы́льной доро́ге, не замеча́я ни жа́ру, ни уста́лости и испы́тывая чу́вство утоле́ния до́лгого страда́ния. Чу́вство э́то бы́ло так ра́достно, что оно́ каза́лось ему́ невероя́тным.

Translation by Constance Garnett, 1901

Fyodor says that Kirillov lives for his belly. That's comprehensible and rational. All of us as rational beings can't do anything else but live for our belly. And all of a sudden the same Fyodor says that one mustn't live for

one's belly, but must live for truth, for God, and at a hint I understand him! And I and millions of men, men who lived ages ago and men living now – peasants, the poor in spirit and the learned, who have thought and written about it, in their obscure words saying the same thing – we are all agreed about this one thing: what we must live for and what is good. I and all men have only one firm, incontestable, clear knowledge, and that knowledge cannot be explained by the reason – it is outside it, and has no causes and can have no effects.

If goodness has causes, it is not goodness; if it has effects, a reward, it is not goodness either. So goodness is outside the chain of cause and effect.

And yet I know it, and we all know it.

[And I looked out for miracles, complained that I did not see a miracle which would convince me. A material miracle would have persuaded me. And here is a miracle, the sole miracle possible, continually existing, surrounding me on all sides, and I never noticed it.]

What could be a greater miracle than that?

Can I have found the solution of it all? Can my sufferings be over?" thought Levin, striding along the dusty road, not noticing the heat nor his weariness, and experiencing a sense of relief from prolonged suffering. This feeling was so delicious that it seemed to him incredible.

The Translator

Constance Garnett is responsible for being the first to make virtually all of the great works of nineteenth century Russian literary prose available to English speakers for the first time. She did this as quickly and accurately as possible, with no background in translation theory and very little of the kind of reference material now available to contemporary translators.

Garnett did have the advantage of speaking English of a vintage nearly identical to that of Tolstoy's Russian. She has been criticized for skipping what she did not understand, for mistranslations and scant attention to matters of style and author's voice, and for excessive Briticisms. Nabokov despised her, calling her translation of *Anna Karenina* "a complete disaster,"

though who can say for sure that he would have had anything better to say about anyone else's?

Garnett went nearly blind while translating *War and Peace* and had to have it read aloud to her. I am in awe of what Garnett accomplished during her lifetime with so few resources and am inclined to consider her sins to be minor. Almost all the monolingual English speakers of my generation who fell in love with Russian literature, and Tolstoy in particular, owe Garnett a debt of gratitude. Readers may decide for themselves whether the above English translation is disastrous.

Commentary

First paragraph: In the second sentence, I would prefer *understandable* to *comprehensible*. It is clear to me that Tolstoy means not that one can see what Fyodor meant, but that people can generally understand the reasons for living like Kirillov. In the third sentence, I find *belly* rather than *bellies* jarring. The choice of *learned* in the long middle sentence is preferable to *wise,* since Tolstoy is clearly referring to philosophers and such, not to those whom he or Levin would actually consider full of wisdom. In the last sentence: *one …knowledge* is unfortunate; most other translators I examined finesse this.

Bracketed passage: Evidently Garnett and the Maudes (Louise and Aylmer, the other highly prolific translators from this era), who followed her, used an earlier Russian version of the novel, which had a somewhat different form of this paragraph in another location in the chapter. I have inserted it here for the sake of completeness.

Last sentence of passage: *delicious* seems an unfortunate mistranslation, but is not fatal to the passage's meaning. However, it is possible an analogous Russian word might have been in the early version of the text Garnett was using.

Translation by Joel Carmichael, 1960

Theodore says that Kirilov the house porter lives for his belly. That's understandable and rational. As rational creatures none of us can live in any other way than for our bellies. Then suddenly this same Theodore says living for your belly is bad, and that you have to live for the truth, for God, and I understand him from a mere hint! And I and millions of people who lived ages ago and are living now, peasants and the poor in spirit, and wise men who've thought and written about this, and said the same thing in their unclear way – we all agree on this one thing: what we should live for, and what it is that's good. There's only one thing I, together with everyone, know with certainty, know clearly and beyond question – and this piece of knowledge cannot be explained by reason – it is beyond that; it has no causes and can have no consequences.

If goodness has a cause, it is no longer goodness; if it has a consequence, it is also not goodness. Consequently, goodness is outside the chain of cause and effect.

It is just this that I know and that we all know.

And I had been seeking miracles; I regretted not having seen a miracle that would have convinced me. And here is a miracle, the only possible one, everlasting, surrounding me on all sides – and I never noticed it!

What miracle can be greater than that!

Can I really have found the solution of everything? Can my suffering really be over now? thought Levin, striding along the dusty road, unaware of either the heat or his fatigue, and with a feeling of relief after long-drawn-out suffering. This feeling gave him so much joy it seemed to him improbable.

The Translator

Joel Carmichael does not appear to have translated any Russian fiction except *Anna Karenina*, although he did produce translations of political works from French and German, as well as Russian. He is known for his

original works on early Christianity, as well as Arab and Russian history. In the introduction to his translation, he does not mince words with respect to his opinion of Tolstoy's style. "[Translating] Tolstoy presents a far simpler problem [than other authors he has just been discussing] for a reason equally simple. He has no style at all. He seems to be stringing statements together so as to convey all the facts needed to make up an unadorned description of real situations. He lacks the slightest interest in using language for its own sake, in order to show off virtuosity. Perhaps his writing is best characterized as flat-footed... It is indeed, just this universal aspect of Tolstoy's style that is so impressive. His flat-footedness means his planting the flat of an immense foot on whatever he wants to say, then pressing it into the reader's mind with irresistible force."

Commentary

First paragraph, first sentence: The identification of Kirilov as a *house porter* is evidently a mistake but an understandable one. The correct word is innkeeper (although *inn* probably has excessively elegant connotations). The Russian word used (дворник) is not defined as anything other than *(house) porter* in any dictionary I know of published in the twentieth century. None of the erudite Russians I consulted had ever heard of it being used for innkeeper. Nevertheless, it appeared in four of the six translations I examined and I finally tracked it down in a facsimile edition of an 1866 dictionary. (Garnett simply did not translate the word.)

Second sentence: Carmichael's is the only one of the six translators who translated both the adjectives in this sentence to my satisfaction. I have already discussed *understandable. Reasonable* (as opposed to Carmichael's *rational)* is a perfectly fine way to translate the Russian word in most contexts, but in English, unlike Russian, it has the additional meaning of acceptable, as in *reasonable price,* or *reasonable request.* Here Tolstoy is specifically and centrally concerned with the opposition between what cold reason tells us and what we feel is acceptable in our souls. Furthermore, at about the time *Anna Karenina* was written, Darwin's works and the

associated philosophy of rational self-interest was much talked about. Living for one's belly is a fairly exact description of this doctrine.

Translation by Richard Pevear and Larissa Volokhonsky, 2000

Fyodor says that Kirillov the innkeeper lives for his belly. That is clear and reasonable. None of us, as reasonable beings, can live otherwise than for our belly. And suddenly the same Fyodor says it's bad to live for the belly and one should live for the truth, for God, and I understand him from a hint! And I and millions of people who lived ages ago and are living now, muzhiks, the poor in spirit and the wise men who have thought and written about it, saying the same thing, in their vague language – we're all agreed on this one thing: what we should live for and what is good. I and all people have only one firm, unquestionable and clear knowledge and this knowledge cannot be explained by reason – it is outside it and has no causes, and can have no consequences.

If the good has a cause, it is no longer the good; if it has a consequence – a reward – it is also not the good. Therefore the good is outside the chain of cause and effect.

And I know it, and we all know it.

But I looked for miracles, I was sorry that I'd never seen a miracle that would convince me. And here it is the only possible miracle, ever existing, surrounding me on all sides and I never noticed it!

What miracle can be greater than that?

Is it possible that I've found the solution to everything? Is it possible that my sufferings are now over? thought Levin, striding along the dusty road, noticing neither heat nor fatigue, and experiencing a feeling of relief after long-suffering. This feeling was so joyful that it seemed incredible to him.

The Translators

Pevear and Volokhonsky, whose translation of *Anna Karenina* was singled out by Oprah Winfrey for sale through her book club, may be

indirectly responsible for progress in teaching the public that not all translations are created equal.

Ms. Volokhonsky speaks native Russian and evidently not good enough English to render Tolstoy; her husband, Pevear, speaks native English and descriptions of his Russian suggest it is somewhere between minimal and limited. The two translate together, using an iterative process until they agree on a version.

In a 2005 *New Yorker* article by David Remnick, *The Translation Wars,* Pevear was quoted as saying "Tolstoy's style is the least interesting thing about him, though it is very peculiar. *Anna Karenina* is interesting very often for how the prose is deliberately not smooth or fine. Tolstoy himself said the point is to get the thing said and then, if he wasn't sure he had said it, he would say it again and again." A later *New York Times* article, (October 14, 2007) quotes Pevear: "It can't be paraphrased; the translator has to follow as closely as possible the exact sequence and pacing of the words in order to catch the 'musical' meaning of the original, which is less apparent than the literal meaning but alone creates the impression Tolstoy intended."

Pevear and Volokhonsky also say that they use the Oxford English dictionary to determine the first usage date of all the words they use, and attempt not to insert many into the translation that only came into usage later.

Commentary

First paragraph, second sentence: The use of *clear* is misleading, seeming to refer to what Fyodor was expressing, rather than the way Kirilov is living. Reasonable, as opposed to rational, also seems a less than ideal choice, as discussed above. Both this translation and the Carmichael one refer to *wise men,* where Tolstoy uses a word that means essentially those who devote themselves to wisdom as a profession, not necessarily those he or Levin admired as truly wise. Garnett's term (*the learned*) was better. In this same sentence, the pair decided to use the Russian word *muzhiki* for peasant,

I suppose to distinguish the Russian subtype from all others. It does not seem necessary to me to introduce the Russian word, which they evidently do throughout. Anyone who has gotten this far in the novel will understand precisely which peasants Levin is talking about, and what Tolstoy considers their salient characteristics. Like Garnett, these translators also use *one… knowledge.*

In the third paragraph (starting with *If the good..*) Pevear and Volokhonsky do something that I like very much, they use the word *good* rather than *goodness.* To my mind, their version is stronger and more appropriate, since both Levin and Tolstoy speak of this concept as of a Platonic form.

Conclusion

This is a very brief passage and it would be foolish to try to draw global conclusions from it about the different translations or translators. Nevertheless, one thing seems to stand out. For all important aspects, the same meaning and the same author's voice come through in all three passages. Given that these were all conscientious translators, the part about general meaning is not surprising.

Given the difference in the statements on this subject by Carmichael and Pevear, and the fact that Garnett would likely have said that she was too busy translating the words to worry about the author's voice, the fact that I, at least, hear the same man speaking is noteworthy. I have pointed out some minor infelicities, as well as felicities, but if you were to add them up, it would be difficult to say that one translation was a great deal superior or inferior to the others. I myself was surprised by this conclusion. I do not claim that it extends to either the entire translated novel or to the talents of the translators involved. Yet it is in keeping with a statement made by Carmichael elsewhere that, "Tolstoy can pull his own weight: his translators merely need to clear the way."

Lev Nikolaevich Tolstoy, 1910

Tolstoy the Outrageous
Возмути́тельный Толсто́й

Tolstoy is rightfully renowned not only as a great artist but as a great and influential seeker of Goodness and Truth. Yet he was also a great rejecter. Today, many of these rejections seem justified, even admirable. These include: immorality, social pretentions, war and violence, eating meat, the greater moral worth of the upper classes, the inheritance of riches and the ostentatious trappings of wealth, etc., etc. Those who know his work well are aware that over the years he spent a fair amount of ink arguing for rejections that many of his contemporary readers found outrageous and many, if not most, people would find so today. We felt that an overview, however brief, of Tolstoy's works and thought would be incomplete without a sample of such opinions.

All translations in this section are by Lydia Razran Stone.

REJECTION 1:
The Influence of Great Men on History

War and Peace, Volume III, Part II, Chapter 28 (1863-69)

It was not Napoleon's orders that caused the soldiers of the French army to set out to kill Russian soldiers at the battle of Borodino. They did this of their own volition. When they saw Russian troops blocking their access to Moscow, the entire army – French, as well as Italian, German, Polish, and Dutch soldiers – all of them hungry, ragged, and weary to death of the campaign, felt that *le vin est tiré et qu`il faut le boire.*[1] If at that point, Napoleon had forbidden them to fight the Russians, they would have killed him and proceeded with the battle – it was inevitable.

When they heard Napoleon's proclamation consoling them for the good chance of them being mutilated or killed, by describing posterity's future admiration for those who fought to take Moscow, they cried *"Vive l'Empereur!,"*… just as they would have cried *"Vive l'Empereur!"*[2] at any nonsense he might have spouted. Indeed, there was nothing else left for them to do but cry *"Vive l'Empereur!"* and go off to fight, so as to get access to the food and rest that would be theirs as conquerors of Moscow. So it was not Napoleon's orders that caused them to kill their fellow men.

Nor was it Napoleon who directed the course of the battle, for none of his troop disposition orders were followed and during the battle he had no idea what was going on around him. It follows that neither the fact that these people killed each other, nor the way in which they did it, occurred in accordance with Napoleon's will, but rather the events of the battle proceeded independently of him, in accordance with the will of hundreds of thousands of people who took part in this mass action. Napoleon only imagined that all this occurred as a result of and in accordance with his will.

----

1. French: "the wine has been decanted and now must be drunk," meaning approximately there is no turning back, or you have made your bed, now you must lie in it.

2. Long live the Emperor (French).

ОТРИЦА́НИЕ 1:
Влия́ние вели́ких люде́й на исто́рию

Война́ и мир, Том III, Часть II, Глава́ 28 (1863-69)

Солда́ты францу́зской а́рмии шли убива́ть ру́сских солда́т в Бороди́нском сраже́нии не всле́дствие приказа́ния Наполео́на, но по со́бственному жела́нию. Вся а́рмия: францу́зы, италья́нцы, не́мцы, поля́ки — голо́дные, обо́рванные и изму́ченные похо́дом, — в виду́ а́рмии, загора́живавшей от них Москву́, чу́вствовали,что *le vin est tire et qu`il faut le boire*. Е́жели бы Наполео́н запрети́л им тепе́рь дра́ться с ру́сскими, они́ бы его́ уби́ли и пошли́ бы дра́ться с ру́сскими, потому́ что э́то бы́ло им необходи́мо.

Когда́ они́ слу́шали прика́з Наполео́на, представля́вшего им за их уве́чья и смерть в утеше́ние слова́ пото́мства о том, что и они́ бы́ли в би́тве под Москво́ю, они́ крича́ли *«Vive l`Empereur!»* ...; то́чно та́к же, как бы они́ крича́ли *«Vive l`Empereur!»* при вся́кой бессмы́слице, кото́рую бы им сказа́ли. Им ничего́ бо́льше не остава́лось де́лать, как крича́ть *«Vive l`Empereur!»* и идти́ дра́ться, чтобы найти́ пи́щу и о́тдых победи́телей в Москве́. Ста́ло быть, не всле́дствие приказа́ния Наполео́на они́ убива́ли себе́ подо́бных.

И не Наполео́н распоряжа́лся хо́дом сраже́нья, потому́ что из диспози́ции его́ ничего́ не́ было испо́лнено и во вре́мя сраже́ния он не знал про то, что происходи́ло впереди́ его́. Ста́ло быть, и то́, каки́м о́бразом э́ти лю́ди убива́ли друг дру́га, происходи́ло не по во́ле Наполео́на, а шло незави́симо от него́, по во́ле со́тен ты́сяч люде́й, уча́ствовавших в о́бщем де́ле. Наполео́ну каза́лось то́лько, что всё де́ло происходи́ло по во́ле его́. И потому́ вопро́с о том, был ли и́ли не́ был

And so the question of whether or not he was suffering from a cold is of no more historic interest than the cold of the lowliest soldier whose task was to carry supplies.[3]

REJECTION 2:
Free Will

War and Peace, Volume III, Part I, Chapter 1 (1863-1869)

Every man lives for himself, using his freedom to attain his own goals. He feels, with every fiber of his being, that at a given moment he can freely choose to perform or not perform one or another action; however, once that particular action is executed, at a certain point in time it is irrevocable and belongs to history, where its significance is of something predestined rather than freely performed.

Every man's life can be viewed from two perspectives: first, as his own individual life, which appears more under the control of his own will the less he is tied to biological needs and the more abstract are his interests; and second, his life as a member of the human beehive as part of which he must inevitably obey the laws laid down for him.

Consciously, man lives for himself, but he is also an unconscious instrument for attainment of the historical and universal goals of humanity. An action once done cannot be undone, and its result, along with the actions of millions of other men occurring at the same time, is of historical significance. The higher a man stands on the social ladder, the more people he is connected to, and the more power he has over others, the more obvious is the predestination and inevitability of his every action.

---

3. Tolstoy starts this chapter saying that various authorities have claimed that the battle of Borodino was lost because Napoleon was suffering from a cold and not thinking as brilliantly as usual.

у Наполео́на на́сморк, не име́ет для исто́рии бо́льшего интере́са, чем вопро́с о на́сморке после́днего фуршта́тского солда́та.

ОТРИЦА́НИЕ 2:
Свобо́дная во́ля

Война́ и мир, Кни́га III, Часть I, Глава́ 1 (1863-1869)

Ка́ждый челове́к живёт для себя́, по́льзуется свобо́дой для достиже́ния свои́х ли́чных це́лей и чу́вствует всем существо́м свои́м, что он мо́жет сейча́с сде́лать и́ли не сде́лать тако́е-то де́йствие; но как ско́ро он сде́лает его́, так де́йствие э́то, совершённое в изве́стный моме́нт вре́мени, стано́вится невозврати́мым и де́лается достоя́нием исто́рии, в кото́рой оно́ име́ет не свобо́дное, а предопределённое значе́ние.

Есть две стороны́ жи́зни в ка́ждом челове́ке: жизнь ли́чная, кото́рая тем бо́лее свобо́дна, чем отвлечённее её интере́сы, и жизнь стихи́йная, роева́я, где челове́к неизбе́жно исполня́ет предпи́санные ему́ зако́ны.

Челове́к созна́тельно живёт для себя́, но слу́жит бессозна́тельным ору́дием для достиже́ния истори́ческих, общечелове́ческих це́лей. Совершённый посту́пок невозврати́м, и де́йствие его́, совпада́я во вре́мени с миллио́нами де́йствий други́х люде́й, получа́ет истори́ческое значе́ние. Чем вы́ше сто́ит челове́к на обще́ственной ле́стнице, чем с бо́льшими людьми́ он свя́зан, тем бо́льше вла́сти он име́ет на други́х люде́й, тем очеви́днее предопределённость и неизбе́жность ка́ждого его́ посту́пка.

REJECTION 3:
Great Art

What is Art? (1897)

Chapter 5

Art is a human activity in which one man consciously by means of certain external signs[4] conveys to others the feelings he has experienced so that these others may be "infected" with these feelings and themselves experience them.

Chapter 7

The concept of beauty not only does not coincide with that of goodness, but actually is more likely to be its opposite, since goodness mainly involves overcoming one's desires and inclinations, while beauty is the basis of all our desires and inclinations.

Chapter 16

Beethoven's Ninth Symphony is considered to be a great work of art. To determine if this is actually the case, I first ask myself whether this work conveys a higher religious emotion. The answer is no, since music, in and of itself, cannot convey such emotions. Next I ask myself whether, although this work does not belong to the highest level of religious art, it yet possesses the second characteristic of good art in our time. Does it have the capacity to unite all people through the experience of a common emotion, so that it can be classified as universal secular art? And again I cannot help answering no, since not only do I not believe that the emotions conveyed by this work can unite people who have not been specially educated to be subject to this complex form of hypnosis, but I also cannot even imagine a group of normal people able to understand anything from this long and intricate

---

4   Earlier in this essay, these signs were specified as involving sounds, visual images, performances and written and spoken language.

ОТРИЦА́НИЕ 3:
Вели́кое иску́сство
Что тако́е иску́сство? (1897)

Глава́ 5

Иску́сство есть де́ятельность челове́ческая, состоя́щая в том, что оди́н челове́к созна́тельно изве́стными вне́шними зна́ками передаёт други́м испы́тываемые им чу́вства, а други́е лю́ди заража́ются э́тими чу́вствами и пережива́ют их.

Глава́ 7

Поня́тие красоты́ не то́лько не совпада́ет с добро́м, но скоре́е противоположно ему́, та́к как добро́ бо́льшею ча́стью совпада́ет с побе́дой над пристра́стиями, красота́ же есть основа́ние всех на́ших пристра́стий.

Глава́ 16

Девя́тая симфо́ния Бетхо́вена счита́ется вели́ким произведе́нием иску́сства. Что́бы прове́рить э́то утвержде́ние, я пре́жде всего́ задаю́ себе́ вопро́с: передаёт ли э́то произведе́ние вы́сшее религио́зное чу́вство? И отвеча́ю отрица́тельно, та́к как му́зыка сама́ по себе́ не мо́жет передава́ть э́тих чувств; и потому́ да́лее спра́шиваю себя́: е́сли произведе́ние э́то не принадлежи́т к вы́сшему разря́ду религио́зного иску́сства, то име́ет ли э́то произведе́ние друго́е сво́йство хоро́шего иску́сства на́шего вре́мени, —сво́йство соединя́ть в одно́м чу́встве всех люде́й, не принадлежи́т ли оно́ к христиа́нскому жите́йскому всеми́рному иску́сству? И не могу́ не отве́тить отрица́тельно, потому́ что не то́лько не ви́жу того́, что́бы чу́вства, передава́емые э́тим произведе́нием, могли́ соедини́ть люде́й, не воспи́танных специа́льно для того́, что́бы подчиня́ться э́той сло́жной гипнотиза́ции, но не могу́ да́же предста́вить себе́ толпу́ норма́льных люде́й, кото́рая могла́ бы поня́ть из э́того дли́нного и запу́танного иску́сственного

work, other than a few short passages that are drowned in a sea of the incomprehensible. Thus, whether I wish to or not, I must conclude that this work is bad art.

It is noteworthy that the last movement of this symphony incorporates a poem by Schiller, which, although obscurely, expresses the idea that an emotion (that of joy) unites people and infuses them with love. Despite the fact that this poem is sung at the conclusion of the symphony, the music does not accord with the theme of the poem, since it (the music) is exclusionary and fails to unite all people, but instead unites only a select few, separating these individuals from all the rest.

REJECTION 4:
Sex

The Kreutzer Sonata, Chapter 11 (1888)

"There are undoubtedly people who have experienced the whole abomination of the honeymoon, but have said nothing [for social reasons]. I too have kept silent, but now I see no reason not to tell the truth… The honeymoon is an awkward, shameful, disgusting and pathetic [ordeal] and most of all boring, incredibly boring. The closest thing I ever experienced was when I was a boy and tried to learn how to smoke, I wanted to vomit… and yet I pretended that I was enjoying it. Enjoyment of smoking, like enjoyment of the other, if it exists at all, comes later; the married couple must train themselves in this vice if they want to enjoy it."

"Whatever do you mean, vice?" I said. "After all you are talking about the most natural human act in the world."

"Natural?" he said. "Natural? No, I tell you, it is the exact opposite. I have come to the conclusion that it is not natural. It is completely unnatural. Just ask small children, or a girl who has not yet lost her innocence. My sister got married very young to a really dissolute man twice her age. I remember how shocked we were on her wedding night

произведе́ния что-нибудь, кро́ме коро́теньких отры́вков, то́нущих в мо́ре непоня́тного. И потому́ во́лей-нево́лей до́лжен заключи́ть, что произведе́ние э́то принадлежи́т к дурно́му иску́сству.

Замеча́тельно при э́том то, что в конце́ э́той симфо́нии присоеди- нено́ стихотворе́ние Ши́ллера, кото́рое хотя́ и не я́сно, но выража́ет и́менно ту мысль, что чу́вство (Ши́ллер говори́т об одно́м чу́встве ра́дости) соединя́ет люде́й и вызыва́ет в них любо́вь. Несмотря́ на то, что стихотворе́ние э́то поётся в конце́ симфо́нии, му́зыка не от- веча́ет мы́сли стихотворе́ния, та́к как му́зыка э́та исключи́тельная и не соединя́ет всех люде́й, а соединя́ет то́лько не́которых, выделя́я их от други́х люде́й.

ОТРИЦА́НИЕ 4:
Секс

Кре́йцерова сона́та, Глава́ 11 (1888)

Так, вероя́тно, быва́ет и с те́ми, кото́рые испыта́ли всю ме́рзость медо́вого ме́сяца и не разочаро́вывают други́х. Я то́же не разоча- ро́вывал никого́, но тепе́рь не ви́жу, почему́ не говори́ть пра́вду.... га́дко, жа́лко и, гла́вное, ску́чно, до невозмо́жности ску́чно! Э́то не́что вро́де того́, что я испы́тывал, когда́ приуча́лся кури́ть, когда́ меня́ тяну́ло рвать ... и де́лал вид, что мне о́чень прия́тно. Наслаж- де́нье от куре́нья, та́к же ка́к и от э́того, е́сли бу́дет, то бу́дет пото́м: на́до, чтоб супру́ги воспита́ли в себе́ э́тот поро́к, для того́ чтоб по- лучи́ть от него́ наслажде́нье.

– Как поро́к? – сказа́л я. – Ведь вы говори́те о са́мом есте́ствен- ном челове́ческом сво́йстве.

– Есте́ственном? – сказа́л он. – Есте́ственном? Нет, я скажу́ вам, напро́тив, что я пришёл к убежде́нию, что э́то не… есте́ственно. Да, соверше́нно не… есте́ственно. Спроси́те у дете́й, спроси́те у не- развращённой де́вушки. Моя́ сестра́ о́чень молода́я вы́шла за́муж за челове́ка вдво́е ста́рше её и развра́тника. Я по́мню, как мы бы́ли

when, pale and in tears, she fled their bedroom, and, her whole body trembling, told us that she couldn't tell us, no she couldn't possibly bring herself to tell us, what he had wanted of her...

"You say it is natural! It is natural to eat. And from the very start of our lives we do it happily, easily, with pleasure, not feeling any embarrassment or shame about it; this other thing is disgusting and shameful and painful. No, it is not natural! I am certain that every young girl who has not been corrupted finds it hateful."

"But how could the human race survive without it?" I asked.

"Ah, yes the human race must survive!" he said with angry irony, as if he had been expecting exactly this familiar and unscrupulous objection. "Preach birth control [for economic reasons as the English do] – and people find that acceptable. Preach birth control for the sake of enhancing pleasure – and that is acceptable. But just try to say one word about abstinence for the sake of morality. And heavens what an outcry it causes." ....

"You ask how the human race would continue... But why does the human race need to continue?" he asked....

"What do you mean why? So we can live." ...

"Why should we live? If there is no purpose, if life is an end in itself, there is no reason to live.... Now if life has a purpose, then it is clear that, when the purpose is attained, life should cease. That follows logically. Note that, if the purpose of humanity is goodness, kindness and love, if the purpose of humanity is what they promise in the prophecies, that all of humanity will be united in love, that the swords will be beat into plowshares, etc., then what is the main impediment to attaining this goal? The answer is passion [worldly desires]. And the passion that is strongest, cruelest and most stubborn – is the sexual, carnal passion, and thus if we eliminate passion and especially the strongest of the passions, carnal love, the prophecy will have come true, people will be united and the goal of humanity will have been achieved, and there is no need for it

удивлены́ в ночь сва́дьбы, когда́ она́, бле́дная и в слеза́х, убежа́ла от него́ и, тряся́сь всем те́лом, говори́ла, что она́ ни за что, ни за что, что она́ не мо́жет да́же сказа́ть того́, чего́ он хоте́л от неё...

Вы говори́те: есте́ственно! Есте́ственно есть. И есть ра́достно, легко́, прия́тно и не сты́дно с са́мого нача́ла; здесь же ме́рзко, и сты́дно, и бо́льно. Нет, э́то неесте́ственно! И де́вушка неиспо́рченная, я убеди́лся, всегда́ ненави́дит э́то.

— Ка́к же, — сказа́л я, — ка́к же бы продолжа́лся род челове́ческий?

— Да во́т как бы не поги́б род челове́ческий! — сказа́л он зло́бно-ирони́чески, как бы ожида́я э́того знако́мого ему́ и недобросо́вестного возраже́ния. — Пропове́дуй воздержа́ние от деторожде́ния во и́мя того́, что́бы англи́йским ло́рдам всегда́ мо́жно бы́ло обжира́ться, — э́то мо́жно. Пропове́дуй воздержа́ние от деторожде́ния во и́мя того́, что́бы бо́льше бы́ло прия́тности, — э́то мо́жно; а заикни́сь то́лько о том, что́бы возде́рживаться от деторожде́ния во и́мя нра́вственности, — ба́тюшки, како́й крик....

— Вы говори́те, род челове́ческий как бу́дет продолжа́ться? ... — Заче́м ему́ продолжа́ться, ро́ду-то челове́ческому? — сказа́л он...

— Как заче́м? Да что́бы жить...

— А жить заче́м? Е́сли нет це́ли никако́й, е́сли жизнь для жи́зни нам да́на, не́зачем жить... Ну, а е́сли есть цель жи́зни, то я́сно, что жизнь должна́ прекрати́ться, когда́ дости́гнется цель. Так оно́ и выхо́дит, — говори́л он с ви́димым волне́нием, очеви́дно о́чень дорожа́ свое́й мы́слью. — Так оно́ и выхо́дит. Вы заме́тьте: е́сли цель челове́чества — бла́го, добро́, любо́вь, как хоти́те; е́сли цель челове́чества есть то, что ска́зано в проро́чествах, что все лю́ди соединя́тся воеди́но любо́вью, что раску́ют ко́пья на серпы́ и та́к да́лее, то ведь достиже́нию э́той це́ли меша́ет что? Меша́ют стра́сти. Из страсте́й са́мая си́льная, и зла́я, и упо́рная — полова́я, пло́тская любо́вь, и потому́ е́сли уничто́жатся стра́сти и после́дняя, са́мая си́льная из них, пло́тская любо́вь, то проро́чество испо́лнится, лю́ди соединя́тся воеди́но, цель челове́чества бу́дет дости́гнута, и ему́ не́зачем

to survive any further. In the meantime, humanity will continue to live, but will have an ideal before them. Of course this will not be the ideal of crocodiles or swine, to multiply themselves to the maximum extent; or of apes or Parisians, to make refined use of the pleasures of sexual passion, but an ideal of goodness, achieved through abstinence and purity. And isn't this what the human race has always strived for?"[5]

---

5. Though this argument is presented by a fictional character and a confessed murderer, in an afterword to this novella Tolstoy voiced agreement with its basic tenets. It is also noteworthy that while Tolstoy, in his 60th year, was working on *The Kreutzer Sonata,* his wife Sofia gave birth to their thirteenth child.

бу́дет жить. Пока́ же челове́чество живёт, пе́ред ним стои́т идеа́л и, разуме́ется, идеа́л не кро́ликов и́ли свине́й, что́бы расплоди́ться как мо́жно бо́льше, и не обезья́н и́ли парижа́н, что́бы как мо́жно утончённее по́льзоваться удово́льствиями полово́й стра́сти, а идеа́л добра́, достига́емый воздержа́нием и чистото́ю. К нему́ всегда́ стреми́лись и стремя́тся лю́ди.

Tolstoy wrote simple and didactic works for two purposes. During several periods when he was resident on his estate, he worked daily teaching peasant children, whom he found enchanting and eager to learn. On the basis of these experiences, he developed a theory of education based on freedom and started to write very simple stories for children, some based on his own childhood experiences, others on traditional fables and some he simply invented. These were collected into primers and were widely used in Russian and even Soviet schools. We include two short samples here. After his spiritual crisis and subsequent conversion, Tolstoy repudiated high literary art (including his own) on moral and religious grounds. He believed that the best art carried morals consistent with religious teaching and should be written in such a way as to be accessible to all readers; an example of this is the third story in this section.

Tolstoy the Didact

How a Peasant Got Rid of a Huge Rock

A very, very big rock lay right in the middle of a town square. The rock took up a great deal of space and got in the way of drivers in the town. The townspeople called in some engineers and asked them how they would get rid of the rock and how much it would cost.

The first engineer said that the rock should be blown to bits with gunpowder and then the pieces carted away and that this would cost 8000 rubles. The second engineer said that a big roller should be put under the rock and the rock rolled away on top of it and that his plan would cost 6000 rubles.

But a peasant who was listening spoke up and said. "Well, I will get rid of that rock and I will charge only 100 rubles."

The people asked him how he would do it and he answered, "I will dig a giant hole right next to the rock; piling the dirt from it on the square; then I will roll the rock into the hole and fill around it with the dirt."

The peasant did what he said he would and they paid him 100 rubles and an extra 100 rubles for having such a good idea.

First published in Russian: 1870
Translation by Lydia Razran Stone

Поуча́ющий Толсто́й

Как мужи́к ка́мень убра́л.

На пло́щади в одно́м го́роде лежа́л огро́мный ка́мень. Ка́мень занима́л мно́го ме́ста и меша́л езде́ по го́роду. Призва́ли инжене́ров и спроси́ли их, как убра́ть э́тот ка́мень и ско́лько э́то бу́дет сто́ить.

Оди́н инжене́р сказа́л, что ка́мень на́до разбива́ть на куски́ по́рохом и пото́м по частя́м свезти́ его́, и что э́то бу́дет сто́ить 8000 рубле́й; друго́й сказа́л, что под ка́мень на́до подвести́ большо́й като́к и на катке́ свезти́ ка́мень, и что э́то бу́дет сто́ить 6000 рубле́й.

А оди́н мужи́к сказа́л: «А я уберу́ ка́мень и возьму́ за э́то 100 рубле́й».

У него́ спроси́ли, как он э́то сде́лает. И он сказа́л: «Я вы́копаю по́дле самого́ ка́мня большу́ю я́му; зе́млю из я́мы развалю́ по пло́щади, свалю́ ка́мень в я́му и заровня́ю землёю».

Мужи́к та́к и сде́лал, и ему́ да́ли 100 рубле́й и ещё 100 рубле́й за у́мную вы́думку.

Bedbugs

I stopped to spend the night at an inn. Before I lay down to sleep, I took the candle and looked into the corners of the bed and at the wall, and when I saw that on all the walls there were bedbugs, I began to consider how I might arrange it that night so that the bedbugs didn't reach me.

I had with me a fold-out bed, but I knew that if I placed it in the middle of the room the bedbugs would crawl down from the walls onto the floor and from the floor onto the legs of the bed and reach me; so then I asked the innkeeper for four wooden bowls, and poured water into the bowls, and each leg of the bed I placed in a bowl of water. I lay down, placed the candle on the floor and began to look at what the bedbugs would do. There were a lot of bedbugs, and they had already scented me: I saw how they crawled along the floor, climbed up the edge of the bowls, and a few fell in the water, and the others turned back.

"I have outwitted you," I thought, "now you won't reach me." I was about to put out the candle – just as I felt something bite me. I looked myself all over: a bedbug! How did he reach me? Not another minute passed and I found another. I began to glance around to figure out how they had got to me.

For a while I couldn't understand how, but finally I glanced up at the ceiling and saw… a bedbug crawling along the ceiling; as soon as he crawled even with the bed, he unhooked from the ceiling and fell on me.

"No," I thought, "you haven't been outwitted!" and put on my coat and went outside.

First published in Russian: 1872
Translation by Robert Blaisdell

Клопы́

Я останови́лся ночева́ть на постоя́лом дворе́. Пре́жде чем ложи́ться спать, я взял свечу́ и посмотре́л углы́ крова́ти и стен, и когда́ увида́л, что во всех угла́х бы́ли клопы́, стал приду́мывать, как бы устро́иться на ночь так, что́бы клопы́ не добра́лись до меня́.

Со мно́ю была́ складна́я крова́ть, но я знал, что, поста́вь я её и посреди́не ко́мнаты, клопы́ сползу́т со стен на пол и с полу́, по но́жкам крова́ти, доберу́тся и до меня́; а потому́ я попроси́л у хозя́ина четы́ре деревя́нные ча́шки, нали́л в ча́шки воды́ и ка́ждую но́жку крова́ти поста́вил в ча́шку с водо́й. Я лёг, поста́вил свечу́ на пол и стал смотре́ть, что бу́дут де́лать клопы́. Клопо́в бы́ло мно́го, и они́ уже́ чу́яли меня́; я ви́дел, как они́ поползли́ по полу́, влеза́ли на край ча́шки, и одни́ па́дали в во́ду, други́е воро́чались наза́д. «Перехитри́л я вас,— поду́мал я,— тепе́рь не доберётесь», и хоте́л уже́ туши́ть свечу́, как вдруг почу́вствовал, что меня́ куса́ет что́-то. Осма́триваюсь: клоп. Как он попа́л ко мне? Не прошло́ мину́ты, я нашёл друго́го. Я стал огля́дываться и допы́тываться, как до меня́ они́ добра́лись.

До́лго я не мог поня́ть, но, наконе́ц, взгляну́л на потоло́к и увида́л — клоп лез по потолку́; как то́лько он допо́лз вро́вень с крова́тью, он отцепи́лся от потолка́ и упа́л на меня́. «Нет,— поду́мал я,— вас не перехитри́шь», наде́л шу́бу и вы́шел на двор.

The Apprentice Devil and the Crust of Bread

A poor peasant went out to plow. Because he ate no breakfast, he took a crust of bread along with him from home. The peasant took his plow from the cart, laid his bread down under a bush, covered it with his coat, and got to work. After a while, the horse got tired and the peasant got hungry, so he propped up the plow, unharnessed the horse and went over to his coat.

The peasant picked up his coat, but there was no crust of bread. He looked and looked, turning the coat this way and that; then he shook it – still no crust of bread. The peasant could not understand it. "What a strange thing," he thought, "I didn't see anyone, but someone took my crust." It was a little apprentice devil who had stolen the crust, and then sat down behind the bush, hoping to hear the peasant mention devils while cursing the thief.

The peasant fretted for a while, then said to himself, "Never mind, I won't die of hunger. Surely the one who took the bread had great need of it. I hope he enjoys it!"

And the peasant went to the well and filled his belly with water, rested a while, caught and harnessed his horse and began to plow again.

The little devil was vexed that he had failed to make the peasant sin, and went off to report to the Head Devil. He told the Head Devil that he had stolen a peasant's crust of bread, but instead of cursing and swearing, the peasant had said, "I hope the one who took it enjoys it." The Head Devil got very angry and said:

"It is your own fault that the peasant got the better of you – you made a mess of things! If the peasants take up that sort of behavior, and their women follow their lead, we're done for. Things cannot be left this way! Off with you! You need to work on that peasant and make up for the crust of bread. If you do not get the better of him in three years I will dunk you in holy water!

The frightened apprentice devil hurried back to earth and started to think about how to make up for his failure. He thought and thought and finally came up with a plan. He turned himself into an ordinary man and went

Как чертёнок краюшку выкупал

Вы́ехал бе́дный мужи́к паха́ть, не за́втракавши, и взял с собо́й из до́ма краю́шку хле́ба. Переверну́л мужи́к соху́, отвяза́л сво́лока, положи́л под куст; ту́т же положи́л краю́шку хле́ба и накры́л кафта́ном. Умори́лась ло́шадь, и проголода́лся мужи́к. Воткну́л мужи́к соху́, отпря́г ло́шадь, пусти́л её корми́ться, а сам пошёл к кафта́ну пообе́дать. По́днял мужи́к кафта́н – нет краю́шки; поиска́л, поиска́л, поверте́л кафта́н, потря́с – нет краю́шки. Удиви́лся мужи́к. «Чу́дное де́ло, – ду́мает. – Не вида́л никого́, а унёс кто́-то краю́шку». А э́то чертёнок, пока́ мужи́к паха́л, утащи́л краю́шку и сел за кусто́м послу́шать, как бу́дет мужи́к руга́ться и его́, чёрта, помина́ть.

Потужи́л мужи́к.

– Ну, да, – говори́т, – не умру́ с го́лоду! Ви́дно, тому́ ну́жно бы́ло, кто её унёс. Пуска́й ест на здоро́вье!

И пошёл мужи́к к коло́дцу, напи́лся воды́, отдохну́л, пойма́л ло́шадь, запря́г и стал опя́ть паха́ть.

Смути́лся чертёнок, что не навёл мужика́ на грех, я пошёл сказа́ться наибо́льшему чёрту. Яви́лся к наибо́льшему и рассказа́л, как он у мужика́ краю́шку унёс, а мужи́к заме́сто того́, чтобы вы́ругаться, сказа́л: «На здоро́вье!» Рассерди́лся наибо́льший дья́вол.

– Ко́ли, – говори́т, – мужи́к в э́том де́ле ве́рха над тобо́ю взял, ты сам в э́том винова́т: не уме́л. Е́сли, – говори́т, – мужики́, а за ни́ми и ба́бы таку́ю пова́дку возьму́т, нам уж не при чём и жить ста́нет. Нельзя́ э́того де́ла так оста́вить! Ступа́й, – говори́т, – опя́ть к мужику́, заслужи́ э́ту краю́шку. Е́сли ты в три го́да сро́ку не возьмёшь ве́рха над мужико́м, я тебя́ в свято́й воде́ вы́купаю!

Испуга́лся чертёнок, побежа́л на зе́млю, стал приду́мывать, как свою́ вину́ заслужи́ть. Ду́мал, ду́мал и приду́мал. Оберну́лся чертёнок до́брым челове́ком и пошёл к бе́дному мужику́

to work as a hired hand for the poor peasant. In a dry season, he told the peasant to sow his grain in a swamp. The peasant listened to his helper and sowed the crop there. The sun burned up the other peasants' crops, but the poor peasants grain grew thick, high and strong. The peasant had enough to eat for the entire year and grain left over besides. In the summer, the hired hand told the peasant to sow his grain on the hillside. That summer was very rainy. Everybody else's crop was flattened by the rain; it rotted and the grain did not ripen, but the poor peasant's crop on the hillside was so good that the stalks could barely hold the weight of the grain. The peasant had a great deal left over. He did not know what to do with all of it.

Then the hired hand taught the peasant how to mash up the grain and distill it into strong drink. So the peasant began to make spirits; he drank it himself and shared it with others. The apprentice devil went to the Head Devil and bragged to his boss that he had made up for the crust of bread. The Head Devil went down to earth to see for himself.

He went up to the peasant's house and saw that peasant had invited over some well-to-do neighbors for a drinking party. His wife was serving the guests, but while she was passing drinks around, she bumped against the table and spilled a glass. The peasant got angry and cursed at his wife.

"You child of the devil, you fool!" he said. "What is this, wash water? You clumsy cow, how can you pour such valuable stuff on the ground?"

The apprentice devil nudged his boss with his elbow. "Just see what has become of the man who did not begrudge a hungry thief his only crust of bread."

The peasant, still swearing at his wife, began to serve the drinks himself. Just then, a poor peasant on his way home from work dropped in, although he had not been invited. He greeted everyone, sat down, and when he saw that everyone was drinking, he began to think that a drink would be just the thing after a hard day of work. He sat there for a long time, his mouth watering, but the host never brought him a drink and was heard to mutter: "Am I supposed to serve drinks to anyone who comes in from the street?"

в работники. И научи́л он мужика́ в сухо́е ле́то посе́ять хлеб в боло́те. Послу́шался мужи́к рабо́тника, посе́ял в боло́те. У други́х мужико́в всё со́лнцем сожгло́, а у бе́дного мужика́ вы́рос хлеб густо́й, высо́кий, колоси́стый. Прокорми́лся мужи́к до но́ви, и оста́лось ещё мно́го хлеба. На ле́то научи́л рабо́тник мужика́ посе́ять хлеб на гора́х. И вы́пало дождли́вое ле́то. У люде́й хлеб повалялся, попре́л и зерна́ не налило́, а у мужика́ на гора́х обло́мный хлеб уроди́лся. Оста́лось у мужика́ ещё бо́льше ли́шнего хлеба. И не зна́ет мужи́к, что с ним де́лать.

И научи́л рабо́тник мужика́ затере́ть хлеб и вино́ кури́ть. Накури́л мужи́к вина́, стал сам пить и други́х пои́ть. Пришёл чертёнок к наибо́льшему и стал хвали́ться, что заслужи́л краю́шку. Пошёл наибо́льший посмотре́ть.

Пришёл к мужику́, ви́дит — созва́л мужи́к богаче́й, вино́м их угоща́ет. Подно́сит хозя́йка вино́ гостя́м. То́лько ста́ла обходи́ть, зацепи́лась за стол, пролила́ стака́н. Рассерди́лся мужи́к, разбрани́л жену́.

— Ишь, — говори́т, — чёртова ду́ра! Ра́зве э́то помо́и, что ты, косола́пая, тако́е добро́ на́земь льёшь?

Толкану́л чертёнок наибо́льшего ло́ктем: «Примеча́й, — говори́т, — как он тепе́рь не пожале́ет краю́шки».

Разбрани́л хозя́ин жену́, стал сам подноси́ть. Прихо́дит с рабо́ты бе́дный мужи́к, незва́ный; поздоро́вался, присе́л, ви́дит — лю́ди вино́ пьют; захоте́лось и ему́ с у́стали винца́ вы́пить. Сиде́л-сиде́л, глота́л-глота́л слюни́, — не поднёс ему́ хозя́ин; то́лько про себя́ пробормота́л: «Ра́зве на всех вас вина́ напасёшься!»

The Head Devil was very pleased at this. But the apprentice devil bragged that this was only the beginning, and there was something even better to come.

The rich peasants drank, and their host drank too. And they began to make insincere, gushing speeches to each other.

The Devil listened to them for a long time and praised his apprentice for this as well; "If this drink turns them into such lying flatterers, soon they will play right into our hands."

"Just wait," said the apprentice devil, "and see what happens next; give them a chance to have one more little drink. Now they are like sly foxes wagging their tails at each other, trying to fool each other; but, you'll see, soon they're going to turn into vicious wolves."

The peasants had another glass each, and began to talk louder and more crudely. Instead of flattering speeches, they began to curse and snarl at each other and then they starting fighting, bloodying each other's noses. Even the host got into a fight and was beaten black and blue.

The Head Devil looked on and liked what he saw. "This is great!" he said.

But his apprentice said, "Just wait – things will get even better. Give them a chance to have a third glass. Now they are raging like wolves, but let them toss down another glass, and they will become like swine."

The peasants had their third glass, and got dead drunk. They muttered and shouted nonsense, not listening to one another.

Then the party began to break up. Some went off alone, some in twos, and some in threes, all of them stumbling and falling down in the street. The host went out to see his guests off and fell face first into a puddle, smearing himself with mud. He just lay there, grunting like a hog.

This pleased the Head Devil even more.

"Well," said he, "you have invented a fine drink, and have more than made up for your failure with the crust of bread. Now tell me what this stuff is made of. You must first have put in fox blood to make the peasants act as sly as foxes. Then, I guess, you added wolf blood: to make them as

Понра́вилось и э́то наибо́льшему чёрту. А чертёнок хва́лится: «Погоди́, то ли ещё бу́дет».

Вы́пили бога́тые мужики́, вы́пил и хозя́ин. Ста́ли они́ все друг к дру́жке подольща́ться, друг дру́жку хвали́ть и ма́сленые облы́жные ре́чи говори́ть.

Послу́шал, послу́шал наибо́льший, – похвали́л и за э́то. «Ко́ли, – говори́т, – от э́того питья́ так лиси́ть бу́дут да друг дру́жку обма́нывать, они́ у нас все в рука́х бу́дут».

– «Погоди́, – говори́т чертёнок, – что да́льше бу́дет; дай они́ по друго́му стака́нчику вы́пьют. Тепе́рь они́, как лиси́цы, друг пе́ред дру́жкой хвоста́ми виля́ют, друг дру́жку обману́ть хотя́т, а погляди́, сейча́с как во́лки злы́е сде́лаются».

Вы́пили мужики́ по друго́му стака́нчику, ста́ла у них речь погро́мче и погрубе́е. Вме́сто ма́сленых рече́й ста́ли они́ руга́ться, ста́ли друг на дру́жку обозля́ться, сцепи́лись дра́ться, исколупа́ли друг дру́жке носы́. Ввяза́лся в дра́ку и хозя́ин, изби́ли и его́.

Погляде́л наибо́льший, и понра́вилось ему́ и э́то.

– Э́то, – говори́т, – хорошо́.

А чертёнок говори́т: «Погоди́, то ли ещё бу́дет! Дай они́ вы́пьют по тре́тьему. Тепе́рь они́ как во́лки остервени́лись, а дай срок, по тре́тьему вы́пьют, сейча́с как сви́ньи сде́лаются».

Вы́пили мужики́ по тре́тьему. Рассолоде́ли совсе́м. Бормо́чут, крича́т са́ми не зна́ют что и друг дру́жку не слу́шают. Пошли́ расходи́ться – кто по́рознь, кто по дво́е, кто по тро́е, – поваля́лись все по у́лицам. Вы́шел провожа́ть госте́й хозя́ин, упа́л но́сом в лу́жу, измаза́лся весь, лежи́т как бо́ров, хрю́кает.

Ещё пу́ще понра́вилось э́то наибо́льшему.

«Ну, – говори́т, – хорошо́ питьё ты вы́думал, заслужи́л краю́шку. Скажи́ ж ты мне, – говори́т, – как ты э́то питьё сде́лал? Не ина́че ты сде́лал, как напусти́л туда́ сперва́ ли́сьей кро́ви: от неё-то мужи́к хи́трый, как лиси́ца, сде́лался. А пото́м – во́лчьей кро́ви: от неё-то

bloodthirsty as wolves. And then you finished off by adding swine blood, to make them act like swine."

"No,' said the apprentice devil, 'that was not what I did at all. All I did was to make sure that the first peasant grew more grain than his family could eat. Men always have the blood of the beasts inside them, but as long as they have only enough grain for their needs, that blood cannot run wild. When he had only just enough, that poor peasant did not begrudge his last crust of bread. But when he had extra grain, he looked for ways of using it to enjoy himself. And I showed him how to enjoy himself with strong drink! And when he began to distill God's gift of grain into spirits for his own pleasure – the blood of the fox, wolf and swine that were in him all along began to run wild. As long as he keeps drinking, he will be a beast forever.

The Head Devil praised his apprentice, forgave him for the crust of bread, and made him one of his senior advisors.

First published in Russian: 1886
Translation by Lydia Razran Stone

он обозли́лся, как волк. А под коне́ц подпусти́л ты, ви́дно, свино́й кро́ви: от неё-то он свиньёй стал».

— Нет, – говори́т чертёнок, – я не та́к сде́лал. Я ему́ всего́ то́лько и сде́лал, что хле́ба ли́шнего зароди́л. Она́, э́та кровь звери́ная, всегда́ в нём живёт, да ей хо́ду нет, когда́ хле́ба с нужду́ рожа́ется. Тогда́ он и после́дней краю́шки не жале́л, а как ста́ли ли́шки от хле́ба остава́ться, стал он придумывать, как бы себя́ поте́шить. И научи́л я его́ поте́хе – вино́ пить. А как стал он Бо́жий дар в вино́ кури́ть для свое́й поте́хи, подняла́сь в нём и ли́сья, и во́лчья, и свина́я кровь. Тепе́рь то́лько бы вино́ пил, всегда́ зве́рем бу́дет.

Похвали́л наибо́льший чертёнка, прости́л его́ за краю́шку хле́ба и у себя́ в ста́рших поста́вил.

This was one of the very last stories Tolstoy wrote. In it we find little trace of his post conversion, simplified style – in many respects it seems a reversion to the style of the great novels and earlier stories. The extreme contrast between the dreamy romantic account of the ball and the horror of the military punishment makes a strong impression. Within the narrative framework, three different philosophical ideas are presented: that individuals on their own determine what is good and what is evil; that environmental influences determine man's sense of morality; and that chance determines everything. Knowing Tolstoy's views about the corrupting influence of society, one might conclude that the narrator's insistence that the story illustrates primarily the role of chance, was included as a means of evading censorship.

After the Ball

"Now you say that an individual cannot, on his own, understand what is good and what is evil; that it is all a matter of environment, that the environment overpowers the individual. But I believe it is all a matter of chance. I am speaking from my own experience."

These words were spoken by our friend Ivan Vasilyevich, whom we all respected, after a group of us had had a conversation on the impossibility of improving the nature of men without first changing the conditions under which they live. No one had actually said that an individual could not on his own understand what is good and what is evil; but Ivan Vasilyevich has the habit of responding to the thoughts a conversation gives rise to in his own mind and then, *a propos* of these thoughts, relating some incident from his own life. Frequently he gets completely carried away by his own story and forgets why he started telling it – especially since his stories are always related with such sincerity and honesty.

And that was what happened now.

"I am speaking from my own experience. My whole life was shaped, not by my environment, but by something quite different."

"What was it?" we asked.

"Oh, that is a long story. To get you to understand, I would have to tell you a great many things."

"Go ahead and tell us."

По́сле ба́ла

— Вот вы говори́те, что челове́к не мо́жет са́м по себе́ поня́ть, что хорошо́, что ду́рно, что всё де́ло в среде́, что среда́ заеда́ет. А я ду́маю, что всё де́ло в слу́чае. Я вот про себя́ скажу́.

Так заговори́л все́ми уважа́емый Ива́н Васи́льевич по́сле разгово́ра, ше́дшего ме́жду на́ми, о том, что для ли́чного совершенство́вания необходи́мо пре́жде измени́ть усло́вия, среди́ кото́рых живу́т лю́ди. Никто́, со́бственно, не говори́л, что нельзя́ самому́ поня́ть, что хорошо́, что ду́рно, но у Ива́на Васи́льевича была́ така́я мане́ра отвеча́ть на свои́ со́бственные, возника́ющие всле́дствие разгово́ра мы́сли и по слу́чаю э́тих мы́слей расска́зывать эпизо́ды из свое́й жи́зни. Ча́сто он соверше́нно забыва́л по́вод, по кото́рому он расска́зывал, увлека́ясь расска́зом, тем бо́лее что расска́зывал он о́чень и́скренно и правди́во.

Так он сде́лал и тепе́рь.

— Я про себя́ скажу́. Вся моя́ жизнь сложи́лась так, а не ина́че, не от среды́, а совсе́м от друго́го.

— От чего́ же? — спроси́ли мы.

— Да э́то дли́нная исто́рия. Что́бы поня́ть, на́до мно́го расска́зывать.

— Вот вы и расскажи́те.

Ivan Vasilyevich thought a little, and shook his head.

"My whole life," he said, "was changed by what happened on one night, or, rather, morning."

"What was it that happened?" someone asked.

"What happened was that I was very much in love. I have fallen in love many times, but this was the greatest love of all. It is all long past now; she has daughters who are already married. I am talking about Varenka B—." Ivan Vasilyevich mentioned her surname. "Even at fifty she is remarkably beautiful; but when she was young, at eighteen, she was exquisite – tall, slender, graceful, and regal. Yes, regal is the word; she always stood very straight, as if she could not do otherwise, and held her head high, which, along with her height and beauty, gave her a queenly air although she was thin, even bony. All this might have been intimidating had it not been for her warm and merry smile, her lovely shining eyes and the youthful sweetness she radiated."

"What glowing terms you use, Ivan Vasilyevich!"

"No matter how glowing they are, they could not begin to give you an adequate idea of what she was like. But all that is beside the point; what I wanted to tell you about happened in the forties. At that time I was a student at a provincial university. I cannot say whether it was a good or a bad thing, but among the students there at that time, there were neither discussion groups nor theories, we were simply young people living according to the nature of youth, we studied and enjoyed ourselves. I was a very lively and fun loving young man, and, furthermore, I was rich. I had a fine pacer horse and used to take the girls sledding (skating had not yet come into fashion) and go out drinking with my comrades. In those days we drank nothing but champagne. If we had no money, we drank nothing at all, but never vodka, as the young do nowadays. Evening parties and balls were my favorite amusements. I danced well and was not ill-favored."

"Come on, don't be modest," interrupted one of the ladies. "We have seen your photograph. Not only were you not ill-favored, you were a handsome devil."

"Well, maybe so, but that's beside the point... What matters is that right when my love for her was at its strongest, on the last day of Shrovetide, I

Ива́н Васи́льевич заду́мался, покача́л голово́й.

– Да, – сказа́л он. – Вся жизнь перемени́лась от одно́й ночи, и́ли скоре́е у́тра.

– Да что́ же бы́ло?

– А бы́ло то, что был я си́льно влюблён. Влюбля́лся я мно́го раз, но э́то была́ са́мая моя́ си́льная любо́вь. Де́ло про́шлое; у неё уже́ до́чери за́мужем. Это была́ Б..., да, Ва́ренька Б..., – Ива́н Васи́льевич назва́л фами́лию. – Она́ и в пятьдеся́т лет была́ замеча́тельная краса́вица. Но в мо́лодости, восемна́дцати лет, была́ преле́стна: высо́кая, стро́йная, грацио́зная и вели́чественная, и́менно вели́чественная. Держа́лась она́ всегда́ необыкнове́нно пря́мо, как бу́дто не могла́ ина́че, отки́нув немно́го наза́д го́лову, и э́то дава́ло ей, с её красото́й и высо́ким ро́стом, несмотря́ на её худобу́, да́же костля́вость, како́й-то ца́рственный вид, кото́рый отпу́гивал бы от неё, е́сли бы не ла́сковая, всегда́ весёлая улы́бка и рта, и преле́стных, блестя́щих глаз, и всего́ её ми́лого, молодо́го существа́.

– Каково́ Ива́н Васи́льевич распи́сывает.

– Да ка́к ни распи́сывай, расписа́ть нельзя́ так, что́бы вы по́няли, кака́я она́ была́. Но не в том де́ло: то, что я хочу́ рассказа́ть, бы́ло в сороковы́х года́х. Был я в то вре́мя студе́нтом в провинциа́льном университе́те. Не зна́ю, хорошо́ ли э́то и́ли ду́рно, но не́ было у нас в то вре́мя в на́шем университе́те никаки́х кружко́в, никаки́х тео́рий, а бы́ли мы про́сто мо́лоды и жи́ли, как сво́йственно мо́лодости: учи́лись и весели́лись. Был я о́чень весёлый и бо́йкий ма́лый, да ещё и бога́тый. Был у меня́ иноходе́ц лихо́й, ката́лся с гор с ба́рышнями (коньки́ ещё не́ были в мо́де), кути́л с това́рищами (в то вре́мя мы ничего́, кро́ме шампа́нского, не пи́ли; не́ было де́нег – ничего́ не пи́ли, но не пи́ли, как тепе́рь, во́дку). Гла́вное же моё удово́льствие составля́ли вечера́ и балы́. Танцева́л я хорошо́ и был не безобра́зен.

– Ну, не́чего скро́мничать, – переби́ла его́ одна́ из собесе́дниц. – Мы ведь зна́ем ваш ещё дагерроти́пный портре́т. Не то́ что не безобра́зен, а вы бы́ли краса́вец.

– Краса́вец так краса́вец, да не в том де́ло. А де́ло в том, что во вре́мя э́той мое́й са́мой си́льной любви́ к ней был я в после́дний день

attended a ball given by the provincial marshal, a good-natured old fellow, rich and hospitable, who had been a court chamberlain. The guests were greeted by his wife, who was as good-natured as he. She was wearing a puce-colored velvet dress, and a diamond tiara, and her old but plump white shoulders and bosom were exposed like in the portraits of Empress Elizabeth. It was a delightful ball. The hall was splendid. There were choruses and music was provided by a then famous band of serfs belonging to a music-loving landowner. The food was sumptuous and champagne flowed like water. Although I was very fond of champagne, I drank nothing that night, for I was drunk on love. On the other hand, I danced till I could barely stand – quadrilles, waltzes and polkas; of course, as many as possible with Varenka. She was wearing a white dress with a pink sash, white satin slippers and white kid gloves, reaching to just below her thin, sharp elbows. The mazurka was stolen from me by that dreadful Anisimov, the engineer – I still have not forgiven him for it. He engaged her for it the moment she arrived, while I had gone to the barber and to get gloves and came late. Thus my official mazurka partner was not Varenka, but a German girl whom I had been somewhat smitten with earlier. But I am afraid that that evening I was very impolite to her, not even looking at her, but instead at the tall graceful figure in the white dress and pink sash, her glowing rosy face with dimples and her warm, lovely eyes. I was not the only one; everyone was looking at her and admiring her, both men and women, although she overshadowed the latter. No one could help admiring her.

"Although I was not her official partner for the mazurka, in actuality I danced with her through nearly all of it. Without embarrassment she would cross the whole hall to pick me as a partner. Without waiting for her to invite me I would leap forward to meet her and she'd smile her thanks at me for having guessed her intention. When she had to choose between a pair of us (by guessing what word I had picked) and guessed wrong, she gave her hand to the other man, and shrugging her thin shoulders, smiled ruefully to console me. Whenever there was a waltz figure in the mazurka, I waltzed with her for a long time, and she, breathing fast and smiling, would say, 'Encore'; and I went on waltzing and waltzing, unconscious of my own body."

ма́сленицы на ба́ле у губе́рнского предводи́теля, добро́душного ста-
ричка́, богача́-хлебосо́ла и камерге́ра. Принима́ла така́я же добро́душ-
ная, ка́к и он, жена́ его́ в ба́рхатном пю́совом пла́тье, в брилья́нтовой
фероньѐрке на голове́ и с откры́тыми ста́рыми, пу́хлыми, бе́лыми пле-
ча́ми и гру́дью, как портре́ты Елизаве́ты Петро́вны. Бал был чуде́с-
ный: за́ла прекра́сная, с хора́ми, музыка́нты – знамени́тые в то вре́мя
крепостны́е поме́щика-люби́теля, буфе́т великоле́пный и разлива́нное
мо́ре шампа́нского. Хоть я и охо́тник был до шампа́нского, но не пил,
потому́ что без вина́ был пьян любо́вью, но зато́ танцева́л до упа́ду
– танцева́л и кадри́ли, и ва́льсы, и по́льки, разуме́ется, наско́лько воз-
мо́жно бы́ло, всё с Ва́ренькой. Она́ была́ в бе́лом пла́тье с ро́зовым
по́ясом и в бе́лых ла́йковых перча́тках, немно́го не доходи́вших до
худы́х, о́стрых локте́й, и в бе́лых а́тласных башмачка́х. Мазу́рку от-
би́ли у меня́: препроти́вный инжене́р Ани́симов – я до́ сих пор не могу́
прости́ть э́то ему́ – пригласи́л её, то́лько что она́ вошла́, а я заезжа́л
к парикма́херу и за перча́тками и опозда́л. Та́к что мазу́рку я танце-
ва́л не с ней, а с одно́й не́мочкой, за кото́рой я немно́жко уха́живал
пре́жде. Но, бою́сь, в э́тот ве́чер был о́чень неучти́в с ней, не смотре́л
на неё, а ви́дел то́лько высо́кую стро́йную фигу́ру в бе́лом пла́тье с
ро́зовым по́ясом, её сия́ющее, зарумя́нившееся с я́мочками лицо́ и
ла́сковые, ми́лые глаза. Не я оди́н, все смотре́ли на неё и любова́лись
е́ю, любова́лись и мужчи́ны, и же́нщины, несмотря́ на то, что она́ зат-
ми́ла их всех. Нельзя́ бы́ло не любова́ться.

По зако́ну, так сказа́ть, мазу́рку я танцева́л не с не́ю, но в действи́-
тельности танцева́л я почти́ всё вре́мя с ней. Она́, не смуща́ясь, че́рез
всю за́лу шла пря́мо ко мне, и я вска́кивал, не дожида́ясь приглаше́-
ния, и она́ улы́бкой благодари́ла меня́ за мою́ дога́дливость. Когда́
нас подводи́ли к ней и она́ не уга́дывала моего́ ка́чества, она́, подава́я
ру́ку не мне, пожима́ла худы́ми плеча́ми и, в знак сожале́ния и утеше́-
ния, улыба́лась мне. Когда́ де́лали фигу́ры мазу́рки ва́льсом, я подо́лгу
вальси́ровал с не́ю, и она́, ча́сто дыша́, улыба́лась и говори́ла мне:
«*Encore*». И я вальси́ровал ещё и ещё и не чу́вствовал своего́ тела.

"Come now, how could you be unconscious of your own body when your arm was around her waist? You must have been conscious, not only of your own, but of hers as well," remarked one of the guests.

Ivan Vasilyevich flushed and almost shouted in his anger, "Isn't that just like all the young people today! You cannot see anything beyond the body. But things were different in our day. The more in love I was, the less I thought about her body. These days you see legs, ankles, and who knows what else; with your eyes you undress the women you are in love with. For me, as Alphonse Karr once said – a good writer by the way – 'the one I loved was always draped in robes of bronze.' We not only didn't undress with our eyes, but we tried to cover up what was naked, like Noah's virtuous son. Oh, well, you wouldn't understand."

"Don't pay any attention to him. What happened next?" one of us said.

"Well, I danced, mainly with her, and had no sense of how time was passing. The musicians kept playing the same mazurka tunes over and over again in desperate exhaustion – you know how it is towards the end of a ball. The papas and mamas were already getting up from the card-tables in the drawing room in anticipation of supper, the lackeys were running back and forth bringing in things. It was after 2:00 a.m. I had to make the most of the minutes that remained. I chose her again for the mazurka, and for the hundredth time we danced across the room.

"'May I engage you for the quadrille after supper?' I said, escorting her to her place.

"'Of course, if my parents do not spirit me away,' she said, with a smile.

"'I won't relinquish you,' I said.

"'Well, relinquish my fan, please,' she said.

"'I hate to part with it,' I said, handing her a rather cheap white fan.

"'Well, here's something to console you,' she plucked a feather out of the fan, and gave it to me.

"I took the feather, and could only express my rapture and gratitude with my eyes. I was not only content and lighthearted, I was happy, blissful; and I was virtuous, I was not myself but had become some being not of this earth, knowing nothing of evil and capable only of good. I hid the feather in my glove, and stood there unable to tear myself away from her. 'Look,

– Ну, как же не чувствовали, я думаю, очень чувствовали, когда обнимали её за талию, не только своё, но и её тело, – сказал один из гостей.

Иван Васильевич вдруг покраснел и сердито закричал почти:

– Да, вот это вы, нынешняя молодёжь. Вы, кроме тела, ничего не видите. В наше время было не так. Чем сильнее я был влюблён, тем бестелеснее становилась для меня она. Вы теперь видите ноги, щиколки и ещё что-то, вы раздеваете женщин, в которых влюблены, для меня же, как говорил Alphonse Karr, хороший был писатель, – на предмете моей любви были всегда бронзовые одежды. Мы не то что раздевали, а старались прикрыть наготу, как добрый сын Ноя. Ну, да вы не поймёте...

– Не слушайте его. Дальше что? – сказал один из нас.

– Да. Так вот танцевал я больше с нею и не видал, как прошло время. Музыканты уж с каким-то отчаянием усталости, знаете, как бывает в конце бала, подхватывали всё тот же мотив мазурки, из гостиных поднялись уже от карточных столов папаши и мамаши, ожидая ужина, лакеи чаще забегали, пронося что-то. Был третий час. Надо было пользоваться последними минутами. Я ещё раз выбрал её, и мы в сотый раз прошли вдоль залы.

– Так после ужина кадриль моя? – сказал я ей, отводя её к месту.

– Разумеется, если меня не увезут, – сказала она, улыбаясь.

– Я не дам, – сказал я.

– Дайте же веер, – сказала она.

– Жалко отдавать, – сказал я, подавая ей белый дешёвенький веер.

– Так вот вам, чтоб вы не жалели, – сказала она, оторвала пёрышко от веера и дала мне.

Я взял пёрышко и только взглядом мог выразить весь свой восторг и благодарность. Я был не только весел и доволен, я был счастлив, блажен, я был добр, я был не я, а какое-то неземное существо, не знающее зла и способное на одно добро. Я спрятал пёрышко в перчатку и стоял, не в силах отойти от неё.

they are trying to persuade Papa to dance,' she said to me, pointing to the tall, imposing figure of her father, a colonel with silver epaulettes, who was standing in the doorway with some ladies.

"'Varenka, come here!' exclaimed our hostess – the lady with the diamond tiara and Empress Elizabeth's shoulders – in a loud voice.

"Varenka went over to them and I followed her.

"'Persuade your father to dance the mazurka with you, *ma chère*.' – 'Oh, please, Petr Vladislavovich,' she said, turning to the colonel.

"Varenka's father was a very handsome, tall, imposing and vigorous old-man. He had a ruddy face, a white moustache curled in the style worn by Nicholas I, white sideburns that touched his mustache and hair combed forward at the temples. He had the same warm, joyful smile as his daughter on his shining eyes and lips. He was very well built with a broad chest thrust forward in the military manner, sparsely decorated with medals, powerful shoulders and long, well-shaped legs. He was a military officer of the type of those who served under Nicholas I.

"When we reached the doorway the colonel was refusing to dance, saying that he had forgotten how. Yet he was smiling and with a graceful gesture took his sword from its sheath and handed it to an obliging young man, and then pulled a suede glove onto his right hand. 'Everything must be done according to the rules,' he said with a smile. He took his daughter's hand, and stood turned slightly toward her, waiting for the music to start.

"At the first sound of the mazurka, he stamped one foot smartly, thrust out the other, and, at first slowly and smoothly, then noisily and vigorously, with much stamping of feet and clicking of heels, his tall, heavy figure moved around the room. Varenka's graceful figure seemed to float around him, the steps of her small, white satin feet effortlessly adjusting to his. Every eye in the hall followed the movements of the pair. I myself did not merely admire them but watched in a rapture of emotion. I was especially touched by his boots – good calfskin boots, but not the type then in style with pointed toes, rather the old-fashioned kind with square toes and low heels. By their looks they had been made by his battalion's shoemaker. *He saves money on boots instead of buying fashionable ones, so that his beloved daughter can be well-dressed and go out in society,* I thought, and these

– Смотри́те, папа́ про́сят танцева́ть, – сказа́ла она́ мне, ука́зывая на высо́кую ста́тную фигу́ру её отца́, полко́вника с сере́бряными эполе́тами, стоя́вшего в дверя́х с хозя́йкой и други́ми да́мами.

– Ва́ренька, поди́те сюда́, – услы́шали мы гро́мкий го́лос хозя́йки в брилья́нтовой фероньѐрке и с елисавети́нскими плеча́ми.

Ва́ренька подошла́ к две́ри, и я за ней.

– Уговори́те, *ma chére*, отца́ пройти́сь с ва́ми. Ну, пожа́луйста, Пётр Владисла́вич, – обрати́лась хозя́йка к полко́внику.

Оте́ц Ва́реньки был о́чень краси́вый, ста́тный, высо́кий и све́жий стари́к. Лицо́ у него́ бы́ло о́чень румя́ное, с бе́лыми *á la Nicolas I* подви́тыми уса́ми, бе́лыми же, подведёнными к уса́м бакенба́рдами и с зачёсанными вперёд висо́чками, и та же ла́сковая, ра́достная улы́бка, ка́к и у до́чери, была́ в его́ блестя́щих глаза́х и губах. Сло́жен он был прекра́сно, с широ́кой, небога́то укра́шенной ордена́ми, выпя́чивающейся по-вое́нному гру́дью, с си́льными плеча́ми и дли́нными стро́йными нога́ми. Он был во́инский нача́льник ти́па ста́рого служа́ки никола́евской вы́правки.

Когда́ мы подошли́ к дверя́м, полко́вник отка́зывался, говоря́, что он разучи́лся танцева́ть, но всё-таки, улыба́ясь, заки́нув на ле́вую сто́рону ру́ку, вы́нул шпа́гу из портупе́и, отдал её услу́жливому молодо́му челове́ку и, натяну́в за́мшевую перча́тку на пра́вую ру́ку, – «на́до всё по зако́ну», – улыба́ясь, сказа́л он, взял ру́ку до́чери и стал в че́тверть оборо́та, выжида́я такт.

Дожда́вшись начала мазу́рочного моти́ва, он бо́йко то́пнул одно́й ного́й, вы́кинул другу́ю, и высо́кая, гру́зная фигу́ра его́ то ти́хо и пла́вно, то шу́мно и бу́рно, с то́потом подо́шв и ноги́ об но́гу, задви́галась вокру́г за́лы. Грацио́зная фигу́ра Ва́реньки плыла́ о́коло него́, незаме́тно, во́время укора́чивая и́ли удлиня́я шаги́ свои́х ма́леньких бе́лых а́тласных но́жек. Вся за́ла следи́ла за ка́ждым движе́нием па́ры. Я же не то́лько любова́лся, но с восто́рженным умиле́нием смотре́л на них. Осо́бенно умили́ли меня́ его́ сапоги́, обтя́нутые штри́пками, – хоро́шие опо́йковые сапоги́, но не мо́дные, с о́стрыми, а стари́нные, с четвероуго́льными носка́ми и без каблуко́в. Очеви́дно, сапоги́ бы́ли постро́ены батальо́нным сапо́жником. «Что́бы вывози́ть и одева́ть

square-toed boots particularly moved me. It was clear that at some point he had been an excellent dancer, but now he was heavy and his legs were not flexible enough for all the pretty and rapid steps that he was trying to execute. But nonetheless he agilely completed two circuits. When, after rapidly spreading his legs and then bringing them together, he fell on one knee, as she, smiling and adjusting her skirt, which he had stepped on, gracefully circled him, everyone applauded loudly. Getting to his feet with some effort, he tenderly and charmingly seized his daughter by the ears and kissing her on the forehead, led her back to me, thinking that I was her mazurka partner. I told him that I did not have that honor.

"'Well, never mind, take a turn with her now,' he said, smiling warmly, as he replaced his sword in its sheath.

"It sometimes happens that the first drop shaken from a bottle is followed by a gush of liquid. In just this way the love in my heart for Varenka freed the great capacity for love that had been hidden in my soul. At that time I loved the whole world. I loved my hostess with her tiara and Elizabethan shoulders, and her husband, and her guests, and her lackeys, and even Anisimov the engineer who was now sulking. As for her father, with his homemade boots and warm smile, so like hers, at that time my feelings were so tender they approached rapture.

"The mazurka ended and the hosts invited their guests to the supper table, but Colonel B. declined, saying that he had to get up early the next morning, and bid his hosts farewell. I was afraid that she would have to leave too, but she and her mother stayed.

"After supper we danced the quadrille I had engaged her for and, even though I had felt infinitely happy before, my happiness continued to increase.

"We spoke not a word about love. I did not ask her, or even myself, whether she loved me. It was enough for me to know that I loved her. I feared only that something might happen to spoil my immense happiness.

"When I got home, I took off my coat, but could not even think about sleeping. In my hand was the feather from her fan as well as an entire glove,

любимую дочь, он не покупает модных сапог, а носит домодельные», — думал я, и эти четвероугольные носки сапог особенно умиляли меня. Видно было, что он когда-то танцевал прекрасно, но теперь был грузен, и ноги уже не были достаточно упруги для всех тех красивых и быстрых па, которые он старался выделывать. Но он всё-таки ловко прошёл два круга. Когда же он, быстро расставив ноги, опять соединил их и, хотя и несколько тяжело, упал на одно колено, а она, улыбаясь и поправляя юбку, которую он зацепил, плавно прошла вокруг него, все громко зааплодировали. С некоторым усилием приподнявшись, он нежно, мило обхватил дочь руками за уши и, поцеловав в лоб, подвёл её ко мне, думая, что я танцую с ней. Я сказал, что не я её кавалер.

— Ну, всё равно, пройдитесь теперь вы с ней, — сказал он, ласково улыбаясь и вдевая шпагу в портупею.

Как бывает, что вслед за одной вылившейся из бутылки каплей содержимое её выливается большими струями, так и в моей душе любовь к Вареньке освободила всю скрытую в моей душе способность любви. Я обнимал в то время весь мир своей любовью. Я любил и хозяйку в фероньерке, с её елисаветинским бюстом, и её мужа, и её гостей, и её лакеев, и даже дувшегося на меня инженера Анисимова. К отцу же её, с его домашними сапогами и ласковой, похожей на неё, улыбкой, я испытывал в то время какое-то восторженно-нежное чувство.

Мазурка кончилась, хозяева просили гостей к ужину, но полковник Б. отказался, сказав, что ему надо завтра рано вставать, и простился с хозяевами. Я было испугался, что и её увезут, но она осталась с матерью.

После ужина я танцевал с нею обещанную кадриль, и, несмотря на то, что был, казалось, бесконечно счастлив, счастье моё всё росло и росло. Мы ничего не говорили о любви. Я не спрашивал ни её, ни себя даже о том, любит ли она меня. Мне достаточно было того, что я любил её. И я боялся только одного, чтобы что-нибудь не испортило моего счастья.

Когда я приехал домой, разделся и подумал о сне, я увидал, что это совершенно невозможно. У меня в руке было пёрышко от её веера и целая её перчатка, которую она дала мне, уезжая, когда садилась в

which she had given me when I helped her into her carriage, seating first her mother and then her. I gazed at these things, and, without needing to close my eyes, I could see her before me at the moment when the mazurka rules dictated that she had to chose between two partners by guessing which description each had chosen. I heard her lovely voice saying "Pride? Right?" as she happily gave me her hand. Or I saw her at dinner as she sipped champagne looking affectionately at me from beneath her brows. But most of all I saw her dancing with her father, as she gracefully circled him and looked at their admiring audience with pride and joy both for herself and for him. And without any intention on my part, the tender feelings I had for her spilled over to encompass both of them.

"At that time I was living with my late brother. My brother generally avoided society and never attended balls, and at that time he was studying for his doctoral exams and led the most regular of lives. He was asleep. I gazed at his head buried in the pillow and half covered by a flannel blanket, and I felt lovingly sorry for him because he did not know and did not share the happiness I was experiencing. Our lackey, Petrusha, met me with a candle and wanted to help me undress but I dismissed him. The sight of his sleepy face and tousled hair touched me. Trying to be quiet, I tiptoed into my room and sat down on the bed. No, I was too happy to sleep. Besides I was hot in the overheated room, and, without taking off my uniform, I quietly went back into the hall, put my coat back on, and went out onto the street.

"I had left the ball after four, and two hours had gone by since then, so that when I went out it was already light. It was the kind of weather typical of Shrovetide, with fog and wet snow melting on the roads and water dripping from all the roofs. The B—s then lived at the edge of town next to a large field, with a parade ground at one end and a school for girls on the other. I walked down our deserted alley onto the main road, where I began to encounter both pedestrians and horse drawn sledges carrying wood, their runners scraping the road. The horses, whose wet heads bobbed up and down under their shiny yokes, the carters draped with mats, splashing along in their huge boots alongside the carts, and the houses of the street,

карету и я подсаживал её мать и потом её. Я смотрел на эти вещи и, не закрывая глаз, видел её перед собой то в ту минуту, когда она, выбирая из двух кавалеров, угадывает моё качество, и слышу её милый голос, когда говорит: «Гордость? да?» — и радостно подаёт мне руку или когда за ужином пригубливает бокал шампанского и исподлобья смотрит на меня ласкающими глазами. Но больше всего я вижу её в паре с отцом, когда она плавно двигается около него и с гордостью и радостью и за себя и за него взглядывает на любующихся зрителей. И я невольно соединяю его и её в одном нежном, умилённом чувстве.

Жили мы тогда одни с покойным братом. Брат и вообще не любил света и не ездил на балы, теперь же готовился к кандидатскому экзамену и вёл самую правильную жизнь. Он спал. Я посмотрел на его уткнутую в подушку и закрытую до половины фланелевым одеялом голову, и мне стало любовно жалко его, жалко за то, что он не знал и не разделял того счастья, которое я испытывал. Крепостной наш лакей Петруша встретил меня со свечой и хотел помочь мне раздеваться, но я отпустил его. Вид его заспанного лица с спутанными волосами показался мне умилительно трогательным. Стараясь не шуметь, я на цыпочках прошёл в свою комнату и сел на постель. Нет, я был слишком счастлив, я не мог спать. Притом мне жарко было в натопленных комнатах, и я, не снимая мундира, потихоньку вышел в переднюю, надел шинель, отворил наружную дверь и вышел на улицу.

С бала я уехал в пятом часу, пока доехал домой, посидел дома, прошло ещё часа два, так что, когда я вышел, уже было светло. Была самая масленичная погода, был туман, насыщенный водою снег таял на дорогах, и со всех крыш капало. Жили Б. тогда на конце города, подле большого поля, на одном конце которого было гулянье, а на другом — девический институт. Я прошёл наш пустынный переулок и вышел на большую улицу, где стали встречаться и пешеходы, и ломовые с дровами на санях, достававших полозьями до мостовой. И лошади, равномерно покачивающие под глянцевитыми дугами мокрыми головами, и покрытые рогожками извозчики, шлёпавшие

which appeared very tall in the fog – all these struck me as particularly attractive and significant.

"When I got to the field where they lived, I saw something big and black at one end near the parade grounds, and from that direction I heard the sounds of fife and drum. My head was always full of singing and from time to time I heard the melodies of the mazurka, but this was something else, harsh, unpleasant music.

"What's going on? I thought, and walked in the direction of the sounds along a slippery path running through the center of the field. When I had gone about a hundred paces, I began to be able to distinguish a number of black human forms through the fog – clearly soldiers. *Most likely a drill,* I thought. And I moved closer, walking behind a blacksmith wearing a greasy coat and an apron and carrying something. Motionless soldiers in black uniforms stood facing each other in two rows, guns pointed downward. Behind them stood the drummer and fife player incessantly repeating the same unpleasant shrill tune.

"'What are they doing?' I asked the blacksmith, who was standing next to me.

"'A Tatar is running the gauntlet for desertion,' said the blacksmith sounding angry, as he stared toward the far end of the ranks..

"I too looked in that direction, and saw a horror approaching between the ranks of men. Toward me stumbled a man, stripped to the waist, tied to the rifles of the two soldiers who were leading him. At his side walked a tall officer in overcoat and cap who seemed familiar to me. His whole body jerking, his feet sloshing through the melting snow, the Tatar, approached as blows fell on him from both sides. At times he would topple backward and the sergeants who were leading him with their rifles would push him forward; then he would fall forward and they would keep him upright, jerking him back. And keeping pace with him, walking with a heavy and spasmodic gait was a tall officer. It was her father with his ruddy face and white mustache.

"As if taken by surprise by each blow, the man turned his face, contorted with pain, toward its source, and baring his white teeth repeated what seemed to be the same few words. I could only hear what they were when

в огро́мных сапога́х по́дле возо́в, и дома́ у́лицы, каза́вшиеся в тума́не о́чень высо́кими, – всё бы́ло мне осо́бенно ми́ло и значи́тельно.

Когда́ я вы́шел на по́ле, где был их дом, я увида́л в конце́ его́, по направле́нию гуля́нья, что́-то большо́е, чёрное и услыха́л доноси́вшиеся отту́да зву́ки флéйты и бараба́на. В душе́ у меня́ всё вре́мя пе́ло и и́зредка слы́шался моти́в мазу́рки. Но э́то была́ кака́я-то друга́я, жёсткая, нехоро́шая му́зыка.

«Что э́то тако́е?» – поду́мал я и по проéзженной посреди́не по́ля ско́льзкой доро́ге пошёл по направле́нию зву́ков. Пройдя́ шаго́в сто, я и́з-за тума́на стал различа́ть мно́го чёрных люде́й. Очеви́дно, солда́ты. «Вéрно, учéнье», – поду́мал я и вме́сте с кузнецо́м в заса́ленном полушу́бке и фа́ртуке, нéсшим что́-то и шéдшим пéредо мной, подошёл бли́же. Солда́ты в чёрных мунди́рах стоя́ли двумя́ ряда́ми друг про́тив дру́га, держа́ ру́жья к ногé, и не дви́гались. Позади́ их стоя́ли бараба́нщик и флéйтщик и не переста́я повторя́ли всё ту же неприя́тную, визгли́вую мело́дию.

– Что э́то они́ де́лают? – спроси́л я у кузнеца́, останови́вшегося ря́дом со мно́ю.

– Тата́рина гоня́ют за побéг, – серди́то сказа́л кузнéц, взгля́дывая в да́льний конéц рядо́в.

Я стал смотре́ть туда́ же и увида́л посреди́ рядо́в что́-то стра́шное, приближа́ющееся ко мне. Приближа́ющееся ко мне был оголённый по по́яс человéк, привя́занный к ру́жьям двух солда́т, кото́рые вели́ его́. Ря́дом с ним шёл высо́кий воéнный в шинéли и фура́жке, фигу́ра кото́рого показа́лась мне знако́мой. Дёргаясь всем тéлом, шлёпая нога́ми по та́лому снегу, нака́зываемый, под сы́павшимися с обéих сторо́н на негó уда́рами, подвига́лся ко мне, то опроки́дываясь наза́д – и тогда́ у́нтер-офицéры, вéдшие его́ за ру́жья, толка́ли его́ вперёд, то па́дая наперёд – и тогда́ у́нтер-офицéры, удéрживая его́ от падéния, тяну́ли его́ наза́д. И не отстава́я от негó, шёл твёрдой, подра́гивающей похо́дкой высо́кий воéнный. Это был её отéц, с свои́м румя́ным лицо́м и бéлыми уса́ми и бакенба́рдами.

При ка́ждом уда́ре нака́зываемый, как бы удивля́ясь, повора́чивал смо́рщенное от страда́ния лицо́ в ту сто́рону, с кото́рой па́дал уда́р, и,

he came quite near. He did not speak them, he gasped them out, 'Brothers, have mercy! Brothers, have mercy!' But his brothers showed no mercy and when the procession got to where I was standing, I saw a soldier opposite me take a decisive step forward and, so fast that it whistled, bring his stick down hard upon the Tatar's back. The man lurched forward, but the sergeants kept him from falling, and then a similar blow fell on him from the other side, and then again from my side, and then from the other. The colonel walked beside him, and looking now at the ground, now at the man being punished, inhaled, puffing out his cheeks and then exhaled slowly between pursed lips. When the procession had passed the spot where I stood, I caught a glimpse of the Tatar's back between the rows of men. It was a thing brightly colored – damp, red and unnatural, which I could not believe was actually the body of a human being.

"'My God!' said the blacksmith standing next to me.

"The procession moved off. The blows continued to fall upon the writhing, stumbling man; the drums continued to beat and the fife to whistle and the tall imposing figure of the colonel continued to move with firm step alongside. Then, suddenly, the colonel stopped, and strode up to one of the soldiers.

"'I'll teach you to hold back,' I heard his furious voice say. 'You think you can just tap him, do you? Do you?' and I saw his powerful hand in its suede glove slap the face of a terrified, weak-looking, undersized soldier for not bringing down his stick hard enough on the bloody red back of the Tatar.

"'Bring fresh sticks!' he shouted, and glancing around, he caught sight of me. Pretending he had not seen me, frowning angrily and with menace, he hastily turned away. I felt so utterly ashamed that I didn't know where to look. It was as if I myself had been caught performing the most shameful possible act. I lowered my eyes, and hurried home. All the way there my head was filled with sounds: either the drum's beat and the fife's whistle or the words 'Brothers, have mercy!' or the colonel's self-assured, furious voice shouting 'You think you can just tap him, do you?' At the same time my heart was full of an almost physical sorrow, to the point of nausea, so that I had to stop several times, feeling that at any moment I would vomit

оскáливая бéлые зýбы, повторя́л какúе-то однú и те же словá. Тóлько когдá он был совсéм блúзко, я расслы́шал э́ти словá. Он не говорúл, а всхлúпывал: «Брáтцы, помилосéрдуйте. Брáтцы, помилосéрдуйте». Но брáтцы не милосéрдовали, и, когдá шéствие совсéм поравня́лось со мнóю, я вúдел, как стоя́вший прóтив меня́ солдáт решúтельно вы́ступил шаг вперёд и, со свúстом взмахнýв пáлкой, сúльно шлёпнул éю по спинé татáрина. Татáрин дёрнулся вперёд, но ýнтер-офицéры удержáли егó, и такóй же удáр упáл на негó с другóй стороны́, и опя́ть с э́той, и опя́ть с той. Полкóвник шёл пóдле, и, погля́дывая то себé под нóги, то на накáзываемого, втя́гивал в себя́ вóздух, раздувáя щёки, и мéдленно выпускáл егó чéрез оттопы́ренную губý. Когдá шéствие миновáло то мéсто, где я стоя́л, я мéльком увидáл мéжду ря́дов спúну накáзываемого. Э́то бы́ло чтó-то такóе пёстрое, мóкрое, крáсное, неес-тéственное, что я не повéрил, чтóбы э́то бы́ло тéло человéка.

– О Гóсподи, – проговорúл пóдле меня́ кузнéц.

Шéствие стáло удаля́ться, всё тáк же пáдали с двух сторóн удáры на спотыкáющегося, кóрчившегося человéка, и всё тáк же бúли барабáны и свистéла флéйта, и всё тáк же твёрдым шáгом двúгалась высóкая, стáтная фигýра полкóвника ря́дом с накáзываемым. Вдруг полкóвник остановúлся и бы́стро приблúзился к одномý из солдáт.

– Я тебé помáжу, – услыхáл я егó гнéвный гóлос. – Бýдешь мá-зать? Бýдешь?

И я вúдел, как он своéй сúльной рукóй в зáмшевой перчáтке бил по лицý испýганного малорóслого, слабосúльного солдáта за то, что он недостáточно сúльно опустúл свою́ пáлку на крáсную спúну татáрина.

– Подáть свéжих шпицрýтенов! – крúкнул он, оглядываясь, и увúдел меня́. Дéлая вид, что он не знáет меня́, он, грóзно и злóбно нахмýрившись, поспéшно отвернýлся. Мне бы́ло до такóй стéпени сты́дно, что, не знáя, кудá смотрéть, как бýдто я был уличён в сáмом посты́дном постýпке, я опустúл глазá и поторопúлся уйтú домóй. Всю дорóгу в ушáх у меня́ то бúла барабáнная дробь и свистéла флéйта, то слы́шались словá: «Брáтцы, помилосéрдуйте», то я слы́шал само-увéренный, гнéвный гóлос полкóвника, кричáщего: «Бýдешь мáзать? Бýдешь?» А мéжду тéм на сéрдце былá почтú физúческая, доходúвшая

up all the horror that had filled me at this sight. I cannot remember how I managed to get home and go to bed. But as soon as I started to fall asleep, I would see and hear the whole thing again, and jerk awake.

"*Doubtless he knows something I do not,* I thought concerning the colonel. *If I knew what he knows, then I should certainly understand what I just saw, and it would not torment me so.*

"But no matter how much I thought about it, I could not understand what it was that the colonel knew. It was evening before I could get to sleep, and then only after I had gone to see a friend and drank with him until I was dead drunk.

"Have you all concluded that I thought that what I saw was an evil act? Not at all. *If it was done with such assurance and was seen by everyone as necessary, then it must be that they knew something I did not,* was what I thought and I kept trying to find out what it was. But no matter how much I tried – even long afterwards, I never was able to find out. And without finding out I could not enter military service as I had been planning. Indeed, not only did I never serve in the military, but I never served the state in any other way, and, as you see, was never of any use to anyone."

"Yes, we know how useless you've been," said one of us. "Why don't you tell us instead how many people would be of no use at all if it hadn't been for you."

"Don't talk nonsense," said Ivan Vasilyevich, with genuine annoyance.

"Well, and what about your love?"

"My love? From that day on it declined. When, as often was the case, she, still smiling, grew pensive, I immediately remembered the colonel on the parade ground and began to feel uncomfortable and distressed, so that I stopped seeing her so often. And my love came to nothing. And things like this do happen, and such things do change and direct a man's whole life. And yet you say..." he concluded.

First published in Russian: 1903
Translation by Lydia Razran Stone

до тошноты́, тоска́, така́я, что я не́сколько раз остана́вливался, и мне каза́лось, что вот-вот меня́ вы́рвет всем тем у́жасом, кото́рый вошёл в меня́ от э́того зре́лища. Не по́мню, как я добра́лся домо́й и лёг. Но то́лько стал засыпа́ть, услыха́л и уви́дел опя́ть всё и вскочи́л.

«Очеви́дно, он что-то зна́ет тако́е, чего́ я не зна́ю, – ду́мал я про полко́вника. – Е́сли бы я знал то, что он зна́ет, я бы понима́л и то, что я ви́дел, и э́то не му́чило бы меня́». Но ско́лько я ни ду́мал, я не мог поня́ть того́, что зна́ет полко́вник, и засну́л то́лько к ве́черу, и то по́сле того́, как пошёл к прия́телю и напи́лся с ним совсе́м пьян.

Что ж, вы ду́маете, что я тогда́ реши́л, что то, что я ви́дел, бы́ло – дурно́е де́ло? Ничу́ть. «Е́сли э́то де́лалось с тако́й уве́ренностью и признава́лось все́ми необходи́мым, то, ста́ло быть, они́ зна́ли что-то тако́е, чего́ я не знал», – ду́мал я и стара́лся узна́ть э́то. Но ско́лько ни стара́лся – и пото́м не мог узна́ть э́того. А не узна́в, не мог поступи́ть в вое́нную слу́жбу, как хоте́л пре́жде, и не то́лько не служи́л в вое́нной, но нигде́ не служи́л и никуда́, как ви́дите, не годи́лся.

– Ну, э́то мы зна́ем, как вы никуда́ не годи́лись, – сказа́л оди́н из нас. – Скажи́те лу́чше: ско́лько бы люде́й никуда́ не годи́лись, ка́бы вас не́ было.

– Ну, э́то уж совсе́м глу́пости, – с и́скренней доса́дой сказа́л Ива́н Васи́льевич.

– Ну, а любо́вь что? – спроси́ли мы.

– Любо́вь? Любо́вь с э́того дня пошла́ на у́быль. Когда́ она́, как э́то ча́сто быва́ло с ней, с улы́бкой на лице́, заду́мывалась, я сейча́с же вспомина́л полко́вника на пло́щади, и мне станови́лось как-то нело́вко и неприя́тно, и я стал ре́же вида́ться с ней. И любо́вь так и сошла́ на нет. Так вот каки́е быва́ют дела́ и от чего́ переменя́ется и направля́ется вся жизнь челове́ка. А вы говори́те... – зако́нчил он.

Tolstoy wrote this story in 1905. The only mention of it in his diary is an entry for February 28: "Have been writing Alyosha. Quite bad. Gave it up." The story was published posthumously in 1911 with several other works of his late, post-conversion period. Prince Dmitry Mirsky in his pioneering survey, *The History of Russian Literature* (1949), regarded the story as a masterpiece. "Concentrated into its six pages… [it] is one of [Tolstoy's] most perfect creations, and one of the few which make one forget the bedrock Luciferianism and pride of the author." The story is indeed remarkable for the simplicity of its language, the austerity of its outline, and the absence of all moralizing that characterizes many of Tolstoy's late works.

Alyosha-the-Pot

ALYOSHA was the younger brother. He was called the Pot, because his mother had once sent him with a pot of milk to the deacon's wife, and he had stumbled against something and broken it. His mother had beaten him, and the children had teased him. Since then he was nicknamed the Pot.

Alyosha was a tiny, thin little fellow, with ears like wings, and a huge nose. "Alyosha has a nose that looks like a dog on a hill!" the children used to call after him. Alyosha went to the village school, but was not good at lessons; besides, there was so little time to learn. His elder brother was in town, working for a merchant, so Alyosha had to help his father from a very early age. When he was no more than six he used to go out with the girls to watch the cows and sheep in the pasture, and a little later he looked after the horses by day and by night. And at twelve years of age he had already begun to plough and to drive the cart. The skill was there though the strength was not. He was always cheerful. Whenever the children made fun of him, he would either laugh or be silent. When his father scolded him he would stand mute and listen attentively, and as soon as the scolding was over would smile and go on with his work.

Алёша Горшо́к

Алёшка был меньшо́й брат. Прозва́ли его́ Горшко́м за то, что мать посла́ла его́ снести́ горшо́к молока́ дья́конице, а он споткну́лся и разби́л горшо́к. Мать поби́ла его́, а ребя́та ста́ли дразни́ть его́ "Горшко́м". Алёшка Горшо́к – та́к и пошло́ ему́ про́звище.

Алёшка был ма́лый худоща́вый, лопоу́хий (у́ши торча́ли, как кры́лья), и нос был большо́й. Ребя́та дразни́ли: "У Алёшки нос, как кобе́ль на бугре́". В дере́вне была́ шко́ла, но гра́мота не дала́сь Алёше, да и не́когда бы́ло учи́ться. Ста́рший брат жил у купца́ в го́роде, и Алёшка сы́змальства стал помога́ть отцу́. Ему́ бы́ло шесть лет, уж он с девчо́нкой-сестро́й ове́ц и коро́ву стере́г на вы́гоне, а ещё подро́с, стал лошаде́й стере́чь и в денно́м и в ночно́м. С двена́дцати лет уж он паха́л и вози́л. Си́лы не́ было, а ухва́тка была́. Всегда́ он был ве́сел. Ребя́та смея́лись над ним; он молча́л ли́бо смея́лся. Если оте́ц руга́л, он молча́л и слу́шал. И как то́лько перестава́ли его́ руга́ть, он улыба́лся и бра́лся за то де́ло, кото́рое бы́ло пе́ред ним.

Alyosha was nineteen when his brother was taken as a soldier. So his father placed him with the merchant as a yard-porter. He was given his brother's old boots, his father's old coat and cap, and was taken to town. Alyosha was delighted with his clothes, but the merchant was not impressed by his appearance.

"I thought you would bring me a man in Simeon's place," he said, scanning Alyosha; "and you've brought me THIS! What's the good of him?"

"He can do everything; look after horses and drive. He's a good one to work. He looks rather thin, but he's tough enough. And he's very willing."

"He looks it. All right; we'll see what we can do with him."

So Alyosha remained at the merchant's.

The family was not a large one. It consisted of the merchant's wife: her old mother: a married son poorly educated who was in his father's business: another son, a learned one who had finished school and entered the University, but having been expelled, was living at home: and a daughter who still went to school.

They did not take to Alyosha at first. He was uncouth, badly dressed, and had no manner, but they soon got used to him. Alyosha worked even better than his brother had done; he was really very willing. They sent him on all sorts of errands, but he did everything quickly and readily, going from one task to another without stopping. And so here, just as at home, all the work was put upon his shoulders. The more he did, the more he was given to do. His mistress, her old mother, the son, the daughter, the clerk, and the cook—all ordered him about, and sent him from one place to another.

"Alyosha, do this! Alyosha, do that! What! have you forgotten, Alyosha? Mind you don't forget, Alyosha!" was heard from morning till night. And Alyosha ran here, looked after this and that, forgot nothing, found time for everything, and was always cheerful.

Алёше было девятнадцать лет, когда брата его взяли в солдаты. И отец поставил Алёшу на место брата к купцу в дворники. Алёше дали сапоги братнины старые, шапку отцовскую и поддёвку и повезли в город. Алёша не мог нарадоваться на свою одежду, но купец остался недоволен видом Алёши.

–Я думал, и точно человека заместо Семёна поставишь, – сказал купец, оглянув Алёшу. – А ты мне какого сопляка привёл. На что он годится?

–Он всё может – и запрячь, и съездить куда, и работать лютой; он только на вид как плетень. А то он жилист.

–Ну уж, видно, погляжу.

–А пуще всего – безответный. Работать завистливый.

–Что с тобой делать. Оставь.

И Алёша стал жить у купца.

Семья у купца была небольшая: хозяйка, старуха мать, старший сын женатый, простого воспитания, с отцом в деле был, и другой сын – учёный, кончил в гимназии и был в университете, да оттуда выгнали, и он жил дома, да ещё дочь – девушка гимназистка.

Сначала Алёшка не понравился – очень уж он был мужиковат, и одет плохо, и обхожденья не было, всем говорил «ты», но скоро привыкли к нему. Служил он ещё лучше брата. Точно был безответный, на все дела его посылали, и всё он делал охотно и скоро, без останова переходя от одного дела к другому. И как дома, так и у купца на Алёшу наваливались все работы. Чем больше он делал, тем больше все на него наваливали дела. Хозяйка, и хозяйская мать, и хозяйская дочь, и хозяйский сын, и приказчик, и кухарка, все то туда, то сюда посылали его, то то, то это заставляли делать. Только и слышно было «Сбегай, брат», или: «Алёша, ты это устрой. – Ты что ж это, Алёшка, забыл, что ль? – Смотри, не забудь, Алёша». И Алёша бегал, устраивал, и смотрел, а не забывал, и всё успевал, и всё улыбался.

His brother's old boots were soon worn out, and his master scolded him for going about in tatters with his toes sticking out. He ordered another pair to be bought for him in the market. Alyosha was delighted with his new boots, but was angry with his feet when they ached at the end of the day after so much running about. And then he was afraid that his father would be annoyed when he came to town for his wages, to find that his master had deducted the cost of the boots.

In the winter Alyosha used to get up before daybreak. He would chop the wood, sweep the yard, feed the cows and horses, light the stoves, clean the boots, prepare the samovars and polish them afterwards; or the clerk would get him to bring up the goods; or the cook would set him to knead the bread and clean the saucepans. Then he was sent to town on various errands, to bring the daughter home from school, or to get some olive oil for the old mother. "Why the devil have you been so long?" first one, then another, would say to him. Why should they go? Alyosha can go. "Alyosha! Alyosha!" And Alyosha ran here and there.

He breakfasted in snatches while he was working, and rarely managed to get his dinner at the proper hour. The cook used to scold him for being late, but she was sorry for him all the same, and would keep something hot for his dinner and supper.

At holiday times there was more work than ever, but Alyosha liked holidays because everybody gave him a tip. Not much certainly, but it would amount up to about sixty kopeks [1s 2d]—his very own money. For Alyosha never set eyes on his wages. His father used to come and take them from the merchant, and only scold Alyosha for wearing out his boots.

When he had saved up two roubles [4s], by the advice of the cook he bought himself a red knitted jacket, and was so happy when he put it on, that he couldn't close his mouth for joy.

Alyosha was not talkative; when he spoke at all, he spoke abruptly, with his head turned away. When told to do anything, or asked if he could do it, he would say yes without the smallest hesitation, and set to work at once.

Сапоги́ бра́тнины он ско́ро разби́л, и хозя́ин разбрани́л его́ за то, что он ходи́л с махра́ми на сапога́х и го́лыми па́льцами, и веле́л купи́ть ему́ но́вые сапоги́ на база́ре. Сапоги́ бы́ли но́вые, и Алёша ра́довался на них, но но́ги у него́ бы́ли всё ста́рые, и они́ к ве́черу ны́ли у него́ от беготни́, и он серди́лся на них. Алёша боя́лся, как бы оте́ц, когда́ прие́дет за него́ получи́ть де́ньги, не оби́делся бы за то, что купе́ц за сапоги́ вы́чтет из жа́лованья.

Встава́л Алёша зимо́й до све́та, коло́л дров, пото́м вымета́л двор, задава́л корм коро́ве, ло́шади, пои́л их. Пото́м топи́л пе́чи, чи́стил сапоги́, одёжу хозя́евам, ста́вил самова́ры, чи́стил их, пото́м ли́бо прика́зчик звал его́ выта́скивать това́р, ли́бо куха́рка прика́зывала ему́ меси́ть те́сто, чи́стить кастрю́ли. Пото́м посыла́ли его́ в го́род, то с запи́ской, то за хозя́йской до́черью в гимна́зию, то за деревя́нным ма́слом для стару́шки. «Где ты пропада́ешь, прокля́тый», – говори́л ему́ то тот, то друго́й. «Что вам сами́м ходи́ть – Алёша сбе́гает. Алёшка! А Алёшка!» И Алёша бе́гал.

За́втракал он на ходу́, а обе́дать ре́дко поспева́л со все́ми. Куха́рка руга́ла его́ за то, что он не со все́ми хо́дит, но всё-таки жале́ла его́ и оставля́ла ему́ горя́чего и к обе́ду и к у́жину. Осо́бенно мно́го рабо́ты быва́ло к пра́здникам и во вре́мя пра́здников. И Алёша ра́довался пра́здникам осо́бенно потому́, что на пра́здники ему́ дава́ли на ча́й хоть и ма́ло, собира́лось копе́ек шестьдеся́т, но всё-таки э́то бы́ли его́ де́ньги. Он мог истра́тить их, как хоте́л. Жа́лованья же своего́ он и в глаза́ не вида́л. Оте́ц приезжа́л, брал у купца́ и то́лько выгова́ривал Алёшке, что он сапоги́ ско́ро растрепа́л.

Когда́ он собра́л два рубля́ э́тих де́нег «нача́йных», то купи́л, по сове́ту куха́рки, кра́сную вя́заную ку́ртку, и когда́ наде́л, то не мог уж свести́ гу́бы от удово́льствия.

Говори́л Алёша ма́ло, и когда́ говори́л, то всегда́ отры́висто и ко́ротко. И когда́ ему́ что прика́зывали сде́лать и́ли спра́шивали, мо́жет ли он сде́лать то и то́, то он всегда́ без мале́йшего колеба́ния говори́л: «Э́то всё мо́жно», – и сейча́с же броса́лся де́лать и де́лал.

Alyosha did not know any prayer; and had forgotten what his mother had taught him. But he prayed just the same, every morning and every evening, prayed with his hands, crossing himself.

He lived like this for about a year and a half, and towards the end of the second year a most startling thing happened to him. He discovered one day, to his great surprise, that, in addition to the relation of usefulness existing between people, there was also another, a peculiar relation of quite a different character. Instead of a man being wanted to clean boots, and go on errands and harness horses, he is not wanted to be of any service at all, but another human being wants to serve him and pet him. Suddenly Alyosha felt he was such a man.

He made this discovery through the cook Ustinia. She was young, had no parents, and worked as hard as Alyosha. He felt for the first time in his life that he—not his services, but he himself—was necessary to another human being. When his mother used to be sorry for him, he had taken no notice of her. It had seemed to him quite natural, as though he were feeling sorry for himself. But here was Ustinia, a perfect stranger, and sorry for him. She would save him some hot porridge, and sit watching him, her chin propped on her bare arm, with the sleeve rolled up, while he was eating it. When he looked at her she would begin to laugh, and he would laugh too.

This was such a new, strange thing to him that it frightened Alyosha. He feared that it might interfere with his work. But he was pleased, nevertheless, and when he glanced at the trousers that Ustinia had mended for him, he would shake his head and smile. He would often think of her while at work, or when running on errands. "A fine girl, Ustinia!" he sometimes exclaimed.

Ustinia used to help him whenever she could, and he helped her. She told him all about her life; how she had lost her parents; how her aunt had taken her in and found a place for her in the town; how the merchant's son had tried to take liberties with her, and how she had rebuffed him. She liked to talk, and Alyosha liked to listen to her. He had heard that peasants who came up to work in the towns frequently got married to servant girls. On one occasion she asked him if his parents intended marrying him soon. He

Моли́тв он никаки́х не знал; как его́ мать учи́ла, он забы́л, а всё-таки моли́лся и у́тром и ве́чером – моли́лся рука́ми, крестя́сь.

Так прожи́л Алёша полтора́ го́да, и тут, во второ́й полови́не второ́го го́да, случи́лось с ним са́мое необыкнове́нное в его́ жи́зни собы́тие. Собы́тие э́то состоя́ло в том, что он, к удивле́нию своему́, узна́л, что, кро́ме тех отноше́ний ме́жду людьми́, кото́рые происхо́дят от нужды́ друг в дру́ге, есть ещё отноше́ния совсе́м осо́бенные: не то чтобы ну́жно бы́ло челове́ку вы́чистить сапоги́, и́ли снести́ поку́пку, и́ли запря́чь ло́шадь, а то, что челове́к так, ни заче́м ну́жен друго́му челове́ку, ну́жно ему́ послужи́ть, его́ приласка́ть, и что он, Алёша, тот са́мый челове́к. Узна́л он че́рез куха́рку Усти́нью. Устю́ша была́ сирота́, молода́я, така́я же работя́щая, как и Алёша. Она́ ста́ла жале́ть Алёшу, и Алёша в пе́рвый раз почу́вствовал, что он, сам он, не его́ услу́ги, а он сам ну́жен друго́му челове́ку. Когда́ мать жале́ла его́, он не замеча́л э́того, ему́ каза́лось, что э́то так и должно́ быть, что э́то всё равно́, как он сам себя́ жале́ет. Но тут вдруг он увида́л, что Усти́нья совсе́м чужа́я, а жале́ет его́, оставля́ет ему́ в горшке́ ка́ши с ма́слом и, когда́ он ест, подпёршись подборо́дком на засу́ченную ру́ку, смо́трит на него́. И он взгля́нет на неё, и она́ засмеётся, и он засмеётся.

Э́то бы́ло так но́во и стра́нно, что снача́ла испуга́ло Алёшу. Он почу́вствовал, что э́то помеша́ет ему́ служи́ть, как он служи́л. Но всё-таки он был рад и, когда́ смотре́л свои́ штаны́, заштопанные Усти́нькой, пока́чивал голово́й и улыба́лся. Ча́сто за рабо́той и́ли на ходу́ он вспомина́л Усти́нью и говори́л: «Ай да Усти́нья!» Усти́нья помога́ла ему́, где могла́, и он помога́л ей. Она́ рассказа́ла ему́ свою́ судьбу́, как она́ осироте́ла, как её тётка взяла́, как отда́ли в го́род, как купе́ческий сын её на глу́пость подгова́ривал и как она́ его́ осади́ла. Она́ люби́ла говори́ть, а ему́ прия́тно бы́ло её слу́шать. Он слыха́л, что в города́х ча́сто быва́ет: каки́е мужики́ в рабо́тниках – же́нятся на куха́рках. И

said that he did not know; that he did not want to marry any of the village girls.

"Have you taken a fancy to some one, then?"

"I would marry you, if you'd be willing."

"Get along with you, Alyosha the Pot; but you've found your tongue, haven't you?" she exclaimed, slapping him on the back with a towel she held in her hand. "Why shouldn't I?"

At Shrovetide Alyosha's father came to town for his wages. It had come to the ears of the merchant's wife that Alyosha wanted to marry Ustinia, and she disapproved of it. "What will be the use of her with a baby?" she thought, and informed her husband.

The merchant gave the old man Alyosha's wages.

"How is my lad getting on?" he asked. "I told you he was willing."

"That's all right, as far as it goes, but he's taken some sort of nonsense into his head. He wants to marry our cook. Now I don't approve of married servants. We won't have them in the house."

"Well, now, who would have thought the fool would think of such a thing?" the old man exclaimed. "But don't you worry. I'll soon settle that."

He went into the kitchen, and sat down at the table waiting for his son. Alyosha was out on an errand, and came back breathless.

"I thought you had some sense in you; but what's this you've taken into your head?" his father began.

"I? Nothing."

"How, nothing? They tell me you want to get married. You shall get married when the time comes. I'll find you a decent wife, not some town hussy."

His father talked and talked, while Alyosha stood still and sighed. When his father had quite finished, Alyosha smiled.

"All right. I'll drop it."

"Now that's what I call sense."

When he was left alone with Ustinia he told her what his father had said. (She had listened at the door.)

оди́н ра́з она́ спроси́ла его́, ско́ро ли его́ же́нят. Он сказа́л, что не зна́ет и что ему́ неохо́та в дере́вне брать.

—Что ж, кого́ пригляде́л? – сказа́ла она́.

—Да я бы тебя́ взял. Пойдёшь, что́ ли?

—Вишь, горшо́к, горшо́к, а как изловчи́лся сказа́ть, – сказа́ла она́, уда́рив его́ ручнико́м по спине́. – Отчего́ же не пойти́?

На ма́сленице стари́к прие́хал в го́род за деньга́ми. Купцо́ва жена́ узна́ла, что Алексе́й заду́мал жени́ться на Усти́нье, и ей не понра́вилось э́то. «Забере́менеет, с ребёнком куда́ она́ годи́тся». Она́ сказа́ла му́жу.

Хозя́ин о́тдал де́ньги Алексе́еву отцу́.

—Что ж, хорошо́ живёт мой-то? – сказа́л мужи́к. – Я говори́л – безотве́тный.

— Безотве́тный-то безотве́тный, да глу́пости заду́мал. Жени́ться взду́мал на куха́рке. А я жена́тых держа́ть не ста́ну. Нам э́то не подходя́ще.

—Дура́к, дура́к, а что́ взду́мал, – сказа́л оте́ц. – Ты не ду́май. Я прикажу́ ему́, чтоб он э́то бро́сил.

Придя́ в ку́хню, оте́ц сел, дожида́ясь сы́на, за стол. Алёша бе́гал по дела́м и, запыха́вшись, верну́лся.

—Я ду́мал, ты пу́тный. А ты что заду́мал? – сказа́л оте́ц.

—Да я ничего́.

—Как ничего́. Жени́ться захоте́л. Я женю́, когда́ вре́мя подойдёт, и женю́ на ком на́до, а не на шлю́хе городско́й.

Оте́ц мно́го говори́л. Алёша стоя́л и вздыха́л. Когда́ оте́ц ко́нчил, Алёша улыбну́лся.

—Что ж, э́то и оста́вить мо́жно.

— То́-то.

Когда́ оте́ц ушёл и он оста́лся оди́н с Усти́ньей, он сказа́л ей (она́ стоя́ла за две́рью и слу́шала, когда́ оте́ц говори́л с сы́ном):

"It's no good; it can't come off. Did you hear? He was angry—won't have it at any price."

Ustinia cried into her apron.

Alyosha shook his head.

"What's to be done? We must do as we're told."

"Well, are you going to give up that nonsense, as your father told you?" his mistress asked, as he was putting up the shutters in the evening.

"To be sure we are," Alyosha replied with a smile, and then burst into tears.

From that day Alyosha went about his work as usual, and no longer talked to Ustinia about their getting married. One day in Lent the clerk told him to clear the snow from the roof. Alyosha climbed on to the roof and swept away all the snow; and, while he was still raking out some frozen lumps from the gutter, his foot slipped and he fell over. Unfortunately he did not fall on the snow, but on a piece of iron over the door. Ustinia came running up, together with the merchant's daughter.

"Have you hurt yourself, Alyosha?"

"Ah! no, it's nothing."

But he could not raise himself when he tried to, and began to smile.

He was taken into the lodge. The doctor arrived, examined him, and asked where he felt the pain.

"I feel it all over," he said. "But it doesn't matter. I'm only afraid master will be annoyed. Father ought to be told."

Alyosha lay in bed for two days, and on the third day they sent for the priest.

"Are you really going to die?" Ustinia asked.

"Of course I am. You can't go on living for ever. You must go when the time comes." Alyosha spoke rapidly as usual. "Thank you, Ustinia. You've been very good to me. What a lucky thing they didn't let us marry! Where should we have been now? It's much better as it is."

–Де́ло на́ше не того́, не вы́шло. Слы́шала? Рассерча́л, не вели́т.

Она́ запла́кала мо́лча в фа́ртук. Алёша щёлкнул языко́м.

–Как не послу́шаешь-то. Ви́дно, броса́ть на́до.

Ве́чером, когда́ купчи́ха позвала́ его́ закры́ть ста́вни, она́ сказа́ла ему́:

–Что ж, послу́шал отца́, бро́сил глу́пости свои́?

–Ви́дно, что бро́сил, – сказа́л Алёша, засмея́лся и ту́т же запла́кал.

С тех по́р Алёша не говори́л бо́льше с Усти́ньей об жени́тьбе и жил по-ста́рому.

Пото́м прика́зчик посла́л его́ счища́ть снег с кры́ши. Он поле́з на кры́шу, счи́стил весь, стал отдира́ть примёрзлый снег у жело́бов, но́ги покати́лись, и он упа́л с лопа́той. На беду́ упа́л он не в снег, а на кры́тый желе́зом вы́ход. Усти́нья подбежа́ла к нему́ и хозя́йская дочь.

–Уши́бся, Алёша?

–Вот ещё, уши́бся. Ничево́.

Он хоте́л встать, но не мог и стал улыба́ться. Его́ снесли́ в дво́рницкую. Пришёл фе́льдшер. Осмотре́л его́ и спроси́л, где бо́льно.

–Бо́льно везде́, да э́то ничево́. То́лько что хозя́ин оби́дится. На́до ба́тюшке посла́ть слух.

Пролежа́л Алёша дво́е су́ток, на тре́тьи посла́ли за попо́м.

–Что же, а́ли помира́ть бу́дешь? – спроси́ла Усти́нья.

–А то что ж? Ра́зве всё и жить бу́дем? Когда́-нибу́дь на́до, – бы́стро, как всегда́, проговори́л Алёша. – Спаси́бо, Устю́ша, что жале́ла меня́. Вот оно́ и лу́чше, что не веле́ли жени́ться, а то́ бы ни к чему́ бы́ло. Тепе́рь всё по-хоро́шему.

When the priest came, he prayed with his bands and with his heart. "As it is good here when you obey and do no harm to others, so it will be there," was the thought within it.

He spoke very little; he only said he was thirsty, and he seemed full of wonder at something.

He lay in wonderment, then stretched himself, and died.

Completed: 1905
First published in Russian: 1911
Translation by Constance Garnett

Моли́лся он с попо́м то́лько рука́ми и се́рдцем. А в се́рдце у него́ бы́ло то, что как здесь хорошо́, ко́ли слу́шаешь и не обижа́ешь, та́к и там хорошо́ бу́дет.

Говори́л он ма́ло. То́лько проси́л пить и всё чему́-то удивля́лся. Удиви́лся чему́-то, потяну́лся и по́мер.

www.ingramcontent.com/pod-product-compliance
Lightning Source LLC
Chambersburg PA
CBHW061455210726
48287CB00007B/2521